I0758037

CONTENTS

ACKNOWLEDGMENT

Artwork and illustration design by Congore, whose visuals helped shape the atmosphere and tone of this story.

Editing, formatting, and cover design by Sienna Arts,
whose work brought clarity, structure, and a finished edge to the book.

Their contributions made The Eggstabletman what it is.

1
FIRST ENCOUNTER

On her 14th birthday, Melody sat in her wheelchair at the back of the tent and watched the magician at his work. His hands quick and clever. The coloured scarves came out of his sleeves like birds, and the crowd laughed. The girl's hands folded in her lap. Her right leg stiff and bent so that her dress skewed against the floor. She looked over her shoulder and nobody was there. Melody squared her frame so no one could see the shame that lived inside of her.

Calliope music played outside the tent, and the scream of fair rides turned the world to dust. The smell of fried dough and manure was there, too. Inside the tent it was dark, and the crowd pressed in close.

The magician produced coins from the air. He tossed them to children in the front row. A small boy clutched a coin like a holy relic.

Melody felt a change in the air. She turned her head and saw a figure step from the curtain at the edge of the stage. A man not tall but strange. His clothes ragged. A hat pulled low over his brow so that only the sharp protrusion of his face showed beneath.

The audience did not stir. The magician did not look.

The figure moved with slow certainty. He took a place at the magician's side as if he had always been there. He inclined his head and looked as if towards her.

She thought perhaps he was part of the act.

The magician cracked a joke, and the crowd's laughter cracked through the ground as though it had erupted from the earth's centre. The figure stood silent. Then he raised one long hand. The fingers narrow and tipped with nails too long. He pointed at the girl.

Melody flinched.

The magician looked about, confused. The crowd followed his eyes, and they found only her. She shifted in her chair, and they stared. A heat rose in her chest.

The figure spoke. His voice was quiet and soft. A whisper. The crowd did not hear. Only she.

"You see me," he said.

She swallowed. "Yes."

"Only you."

Melody's heart thudded.

She looked around for confirmation, but the crowd was already restless. The magician stretched his painted smile and spread his hands. A trick gone wrong. He turned it into comedy. The attention slid away from her, and the laughter returned.

But the figure did not vanish. His voice came as though he were leaning in to speak into her ear. She didn't hear a single breath.

"Do you wish to dance?"

She did not answer.

"I can teach you."

And she closed her eyes. She did not open them, not until she felt her mother sit beside her.

"What did I miss?" she asked.

But Melody kept quiet.

At home she sat by the sofa watching her brother Ford draw. When he put crayon to paper, the world vanished from around him. Melody remained. She knew it from the way he turned to look at her and only her. Nobody else.

The TV played the news. The voices spoke of a cure for HIV. There was talk of a new operation that could make teeth grow forever. Hair, too. They've finally found a method to travel to the Moon and stay there. They even found a way to create biodegradable plastic. In truth, the talk only made brief mention of these advancements. Most words were reserved for the strange coincidence linking them all: those responsible had gone missing the day after making their discoveries public. Conspiracy theories sprang out and lay like fog over the world. Little Ashland, a small Saunders County city in Nebraska, had not been spared.

"It's better off they don't come out with these things anymore," India's voice came from the kitchen. "Sure, the world needs them, but I couldn't fathom losing anyone like that."

Melody's mother sauntered into the threshold between kitchen and living room. She lingered. Her eyes rested on her son, briefly. Melody met her gaze and smiled.

"It's Baller," India whispered. "Do you want to say hi to your brother?"

Melody nodded.

"Just a minute now honey, Melody wants to say hi."

India paced across the room. She stepped over Ford and passed the phone to the girl.

"Melody?"

"Hi Bally, How's things?"

"Not too bad. Summer's coming in good here in Cali. How about you?"

"Been to the circus today with Mom."

"How was it?"

She opened her mouth to speak of the rides and food and all of the mud that caked the wheels of her wheelchair, but as though a wrench had been thrown into the cogs of her brain, all she could see when thinking of today was the odd figure standing and swaying next to the magician. It did not have a face. Only a voice. A soft whisper invading her.

"Melody?" Her brother pulled her out.

"It was alright," she said looking up at her mother. India smiled, her head tilted. "It Would've been better if you were there." And she meant it. With Baller at her side, Melody felt invincible.

"Come on, now, don't say that. Don't make me feel bad. What about Ford? Why didn't the rascal come?"

Melody shook her head. "He wanted to help Dad out on the farm."

"Did he now? Why, I never woulda thought."

India tapped her fingers on the hem of her dress. "Mom wants you back."

"Alright, well you take care of yourself, okay? I'll be back home before you know it."

"When's that?"

Baller hesitated. "I don't know, Mel. Soon enough. You hang in there and look after Little Fordie, alright?"

"Okay. Love you."

"Love you too, Mel."

She passed the phone back to her mother. "Right," India said, stepping back over Ford and heading into the kitchen. "As I was saying, I just can't imagine it. You better not go into any of those scientific fields, Ball. You better not. I don't care."

Melody sat with her hands crossed in her lap. She turned her head to look out the window. Two girls her age walked hand in hand. At times they skipped and ran and laughed so much that she had to look away. A throb rose in her twisted foot. She pinched her dress and pulled it lower to hide herself.

"Don't do that," Ford said.

"Leave me alone."

Ford shook his head. "I like your foot, Mel. It gives you powers."

"It doesn't," she tutted. "What powers do I have?"

"You're like, totally awesome," he said and meant it. A glow like a newborn star was there in his eyes. "Look." He lifted the piece of paper he had been sketching on.

"Why does my wheelchair have a cape?"

"You're a hero!" he smiled.

"It doesn't look like I am the hero in that," she said, rolling herself a little closer and taking the picture in her hand. His smile was too bright. "But it's great. I love it."

"You don't have to lie."

"I'm not."

"I'll draw a better one. I promise. I just got the idea now. I didn't think too much about it."

"It's okay, Ford. I mean it."

The boy shook his head. "You'll see. I draw you great and—"

The front door came open. Heavy steps dragged into the hall.

"Ford? Ford, where are you?" Victor's voice spilled into the house.

"Here, Pops. What's the matter?"

"Come and give me a hand with the watering. My back's all done for the day. Here," he stepped into the threshold. He was all covered in dirt and held an empty bucket in his hand. "Take this and let's go."

Ford jumped to his feet and rushed to his father. "Just need to put on my rubber boots."

After a short hug, Ford took the bucket from his hands and disappeared into the hall.

"Hey there," Victor awkwardly waved at her. Melody smiled. "All good?"

"All good," she nodded.

"Great," he hesitated. He swung from toe to heel. His eyes looked around her, only briefly catching a glance at her face and condition. "You tell me if you need anything, okay? Tell your mother."

"I know."

A curt nod took him back out of the house. He closed the door in his wake, and the house was silent with life. Her mother whispered on the phone to her brother somewhere far. The news was still on. Going on forever.

She was tired.

That night she lay in her bed in the farmhouse at the edge of town and dreamt a sort of real haze. She was once more in the tent at the circus. Only the people were gone. The seats were empty. The magician is nowhere to be seen.

The figure stood alone on the stage. He was surrounded by large eggs laid still on their sides. Eggs large enough to fit a human. The figure swung on his bare feet. He was four-toed. Long claws like hooks stabbed into the boards. The voice came again, and this time around it spoke from everywhere, as if already in her head. She could not tell what it said.

The figure looked up. The brim of its hat no longer covered its eyes. They were red like burning coal. The rest of his face was lost in shadow.

She wanted to pull away but couldn't. The amber air of dreams made her moveless.

The figure stepped forward. He stepped down from the stage and came to her all the way in the back. He extended his hand. His four fingers - long and cold.

The girl shook her head.

"You are broken," the figure said. The words were close to her mind. She felt them sliding over and into the back. "But you need not remain so."

She blinked, and the figure was gone. Only the eggs remained now on stage. She listened as though they could speak, and for a moment she heard something akin to broken voices. They cried out for her, or so it seemed. From outside came a scream. It startled her, and yet she could not move but only listen. The scream grew louder. Until she felt it in her throat.

"Mel!" The bang of the door woke her up. The light came on, and Victor stood there with a revolver in his hand. Hammer cocked.

He paced the room and scanned. Her mother rushed to her side and took her in her arms.

"You're okay," she embraced her. "You're alright."

Melody's heart raced. She heaved. She watched her father at the periphery of her vision as he came to a stop. He lowered the revolver and watched her with a frown on his face. Sleep kissed his features, though the effect was wearing off.

"Need me to stay here with you?" he asked.

"No."

"You sure?"

The girl nodded. "It was just a bad dream."

"You tell me and I'll stay. Don't go shy on me."

"I'm fine, Dad. I don't need you guys babying me."

"I'm just saying," he scratched his face. "Tell her, India. Tell her I ain't mean it like that."

"You know how your father is, sweetie," India looked into her daughter's face. "He just wants to be sure."

"Would you act the same if I didn't have this leg of mine?"

Victor resigned himself to her question. He drew back into the hall without a word. Her mother stood and watched her for a moment. Then another.

"Good night," she said. "You call us if anything."

She flicked the light off and left the door ever-so-slightly ajar.

Melody closed her eyes in play-pretend knowing that sleep would come no more. At least not that night.

The following morning stitched itself to many others as though time had decided to speed up. Odd glances slipped her way from her parents. They had never been there before, but they were there now. Only Ford remained the same. Each morning he made sure to show her a new drawing. That very first one after the nightmare was a readjustment of the one he had previously shown her. This time, the cape was on her back.

"Much better," Melody said.

Ford pushed her from the bus stop and all the way to the school each morning. By the time they reached the gates, she told him to let off as she didn't want the other children to see her younger brother doing such a thing. Ford didn't mind but let off anyway.

She put it down to the nightmare that things seemed to take a darker turn as the months rolled on. In the halls, the girls pulled away from her and turned their heads to whisper dark secrets. Boys were simpler. Straighter. They snickered and pointed fingers. On one of the worst days, a guy one year her senior rushed in front of her and started dragging his right leg across the floor. He rolled his eyes and groaned mindlessly.

"What am I?" he asked, half-mouthed. "A zombie?"

"You're me," she said, pursing her lips.

"Fuck yeah, I am," he cackled. And the rest did too. Boys came and hit his arm and ruffled his hair all the while pointing fingers at her and adding to the bit. "Freak."

At times, Ford came to her side and stood against them. More often than not, it left him with a black eye or busted lip.

"You don't have to do all that for me, Ford."

"I know I don't, but I wanna," he said.

"Well, you don't have to wanna. I don't want you to."

He was wheeling her to the bus stop, heading home, in spring. Thanksgiving and Christmas and New Year's had passed and Baller didn't come home. He had lied to her. Abandoned her to the world. Ford ended up being the only thing she still had.

"Why can't I wanna?" Ford asked. He had let his hair grow long, and whenever it got in his eyes for too long, he stopped pushing her to push the strands aside. "It's not up to you."

"It's enough that they hate me. I don't want them to hate you too."

The boy pushed her along, drawing out the silence. "Whatever," he said in the end.

They waited for the bus to come. The wind spoke in calm susurration with the leaves of distant trees, drawing the silence to a close. The bus hissed into the station, and Ford struggled without the aid of his father to help Melody onto the bus. He was still too small for it all.

The figure had not shown itself to her again since her nightmare that summer. Not until the end of spring. Melody had spent most of that Saturday outside. It was unlike her. She much preferred to be indoors with her nose in some book or watching her brother draw. Whether that was due to her condition or because she truly enjoyed those activities, she had no power to know.

It was getting dark. The sun spilled its last rays of light onto the sky. They dragged and grew heavy and fell beyond the horizon, leaving space only for a purple tinge to spread over the sky.

Her parents were sure to come looking for her. She never stayed out that late. Perhaps because of this, she ventured out into the woods. To be free a little longer.

She wheeled herself through dirt and foliage and listened to the snap of twigs beneath her. A chirp in the distance. It was not natural. The birds retreated this late. She turned towards it to meander through the trees, finding her way into the wash of a chant, ushering her along.

The dark thickened, but in the distance a spit of light remained and flickered. She drew closer. The chant possessed a chopped rhythm. The words were carved out of young lips coming together. She wheeled herself behind a tree and listened.

> *Low hat. Long hands.*
> *Soft voice. Still stands.*
> *Grey Skin. Red eyes.*
> *Walks dark. Eats lives.*
> *Four steps. Four nails.*
> *One smile. One veil.*
> *Count years. Count time.*
> *At twenty-nine, you're mine.*

The group moved like shadows around the campfire. Melody thought she recognized a few faces from school but could not tell for certain. She was too far away, and the light did not play in her favour.

"Have any of you seen it yet?" a girl asked once they were done with the song.

"Betty has," a boy responded.

"Betty?"

They all turned to her. Melody too. Betty was in the same class as her younger brother. She pulled at her shirt and kept her eyes to the ground.

"She has *not*! Otherwise, she would've told us."

"She told me," the same boy from before responded. "Come on, Betty. Don't be shy."

Betty shook her head. "I'm scared."

"That's good. Why wouldn't you be?"

"He's scary," Betty whimpered. "I don't—"

"I don't believe you," another girl shook her head. "My brother said it's not that bad. There's nothing to be scared of."

"Well, *I'm* scared."

"You're lying."

"I'm not lying! I've seen him!" Betty shouted. "I've seen the Eggstabletman. He's come to me in a dream!"

The only sound was that of the fire crackling. Melody sat with her heart thumping in her throat when the figure pulled out of the dark. Its steps were slow. Mute. It drew close to Betty, swinging from side to side. The children were not aware of it. Its eyes no longer burned. They were hollow and dark like the rest of its face.

"And what did he say to you?"

"He screamed at me!"

"Bullshit! The Eggstabletman doesn't scream. He whispers!"

"That's right," a boy nodded. "That's what everyone says."

"Well, to me he screamed! There's not only one, right? There's many all over the world."

"Stop making stuff up Betty. It's not cool. You can lose your membership for that."

The girl looked up in agony. "I'm not lying, I swear. I—I've seen him. Please. Don't kick me out. The 20s Club is all I have. Please."

"What are you hiding from?" The figure's voice rang inside of her head. "Are you scared, little girl?"

Melody clutched at her wheels.

"You want to run?" it whispered. "Are you sure? Shouldn't you stay and hear more?"

She turned halfway.

"Where are you going? You can't run. Not without me."

She wanted to scream. She could not. The others would be alerted.

"Stay, stay," the figure beckoned. Melody looked away completely. She did not want to see. Yet she felt it. It was closer. It was there. She could smell it. It was all inside of her nose. This strange scent of nothing and everything all together. "Stay so you can hear more about me. Don't you want to know what I can do?"

The figure's long nails wrapped around Melody's head. They pushed out from behind her and closed in like a cage. She tensed up and yanked at the wheels. She skidded and spun on the spot by accident instead of bolting away. Foliage hissed beneath her.

"AAAAAAAAAH!" Betty screeched.

"What was that?"

"Fuck! Who's there?"

The group huddled together. Girls covered their faces while boys picked up sticks and rocks, and one even held his father's pistol. His finger shook on the trigger. They all held their breaths. The fire, too, kept quiet. They stared into the dark. Searching for the sound. The fire did not stretch its hands of light far enough. They could not see. Fear was all they had and it tightened around them.

"Wh-wh-what if it's the—"

"Betty, shut the fuck up!" the boy holding the pistol hissed. "Shut up!"

"Sorry, I—"

Pop!

Firewood snapped.

"Shit!" The boy tensed his finger and shot. A burst lit up the surroundings. The bullet flew and cut the side of a tree and went past it, sinking into the dark, "It's there!" he said "Fuck! It's there! Shit!"

"Kill it, Sam! Kill it! Shoot!"

And the boy shot. Again and again and again, with the flash of the muzzle like starlight, until the clip was empty.

"Did you get it?"

"I—I don't know," Sam held the pistol pointed at the dark.

"Go check."

"I'm not going," he shook his head. "I shot it. I'm not going. That's not fair."

"Then someone else go."

"Send a girl."

"A boy!" the girls roared in a chorus. "You all go. You have weapons."

The boys looked at one another, uncertain. Fear draped over them, and even with it, they got close together and moved forward. Sticks and rocks and an empty pistol. They lingered on the edge of the light and hesitated to step further into the dark.

A gale of wind rushed through and carried with it a set of fallen leaves. It swirled them around the fire, and the girls began to scream of ghosts and banshees and curses. The boys turned, half-way swallowed by the dark. Some threw their rocks at the tornado. Others held onto them in fear.

Betty covered her face with her hands. "I'm sorry. I'm sorry!" she whimpered. "I didn't mean to tell about you! I didn't mean to! I'm sorry!"

A noise came from behind the boys. From within the dark's jaws. It broke their formation and made them scatter. They left the girls behind. As soon as they saw they were alone, they ran too. Only Betty remained. She kept her hands over her face as she curled into herself.

She sat there until the fire ran out. Until dawn cracked its shell over the world to engulf it in its light.

Betty was declared missing that very morning.

Victor paced to and fro in the kitchen with his hands akimbo. He shook his head, looked at the ground, turned to Melody, looked back at the ground, and then paced again. India sat next to her. On the table there was a bowl filled with warm water. Her mother dipped a cloth in there, wrung it, and brushed gently at the cut stretching from Melody's temple to the back of her ear.

"Just tell me one thing honey, that's all I want," her father said. "Why the *hell*—"

"Victor!" India stopped her hand for a second to correct him.

"Why go into the woods?" He lowered his voice. "Why at all?"

Melody said nothing.

"There's no reason for you to keep hold of that rascal's name that shot you. No reason!"

He stopped again to look at her. He opened his mouth but the words didn't come. Slow, light footsteps traced into the kitchen. Ford rubbed his eyes with both hands and made sure to be heard with a loud yawn.

"What's got you out of bed at this hour on a Sunday?" Victor asked.

"You're shouting. I can't sleep."

Victor bit his lower lip and nodded. "I'll keep it down. Go back to bed."

Ford's eyes were small and squinted. Sleep resisted his attempts at brushing it away from his lids. When he looked at his sister, he only saw the blur of her face and not the whole thing.

"Why's Mel awake? Is she in trouble?"

India shot Victor a look. He was inspired enough to turn to her before giving a response. The mother subtly shook her head.

"No she's not in trouble. We're just talking."

"This loud?"

"You know how I am, boy. Sometimes I can't help it," Victor picked the boy up and slung him over his shoulder. "I'm taking you right back."

Ford did not resist. He caught one last look at his sister as his father turned the corner with him. A clearer look.

"Are you sure she's not in trouble?" Ford whispered.

"I'm sure."

"Well, is she alright, at least, Pap?"

Victor hesitated. "She's okay, son. Nothing for you to worry about." He dropped the boy into bed and threw the covers over him. "You go back to sleep, alright? If I wake you up again, you let me know at noon, and I'll make it up to you."

"You'll let me draw you?"

"Sure, son. Why not?"

Victor left Little Fordie behind with a smile as he drifted back into sleep. Once he was back down in the kitchen, he found his daughter crying.

"What's the matter? What did you say to her?"

India shook her head. "She just started crying. Sweetie, what is it?"

Victor sat down. He laced his fingers together. He tightened them. His bones cracked. He scratched the side of his face and looked out the window. In the distance, some elm tree swung back and forth and lost its colour.

"You don't have to tell us a thing," he said. "I just need to know that you're alright. You hear? Not a single thing. I don't care about no rascal. I don't care about his pistol and how he got the damn thing. I only care about you. From the very beginning, this was about you." He stopped a moment to watch a neighbour take her dog out for a walk. "Maybe I made it seem like it wasn't. But it is." He looked at his wife for support. Her arms were around Melody. She caressed her with gentle motions that seemed to be more attempts at ushering her out of her shell. "Are you curious about the forest?"

Melody shook her head.

"The outside world, then?"

Again.

"Then I don't know," Victor sighed. "Look. I'm willing to take time out of my day to come with you wherever you want to go. But not like this. Not alone."

"I'm old enough," Melody muttered.

"Sure you are," he said. "But not old enough to get shot. It ain't right."

"But you said—"

"I know what I said, and I'm keeping to it. I'll find out about that boy and deal with it myself. It'll have nothing to do with you."

"Do you want to take a few days off school?" India asked.

"No."

"Are you sure? Don't you feel weak?"

"It's just a scratch," Melody said. "I don't feel any worse than I usually do."

India and Victor exchanged glances. Victor shrugged and stood up. "I'm going out. Give me a shout if the world comes falling down."

They watched him leave. The lack of his presence dipped them in silence.

A Talent Show had been scheduled for Monday after class. Melody had forgotten all about it, much like she did with the others before it. With her condition, she never felt as if she would ever be able to get up on that stage and show the school anything worthy of seeing. Perhaps a comedic bit where she could sit there and let them laugh at her. But she didn't hate herself that much.

As soon as she got to school, it was clear that the classes were not going to last. All the talk was of Betty. Tales already spread of the girl having been a nymph. People pretended to forget about her existence in school although others pointed at pictures of her in the yearbooks. Girls claimed magic while boys made mention of devilish things.

Melody knew it was nothing of the sort. In her first and only period of the day, she looked out the window and through it she found herself back in the forest watching the group of children around the campfire. One by one they disappeared, leaving only Betty behind. She tried to approach the girl with her gaze, but she sat down on the foliage and brought her knees to her chest. She sank her face in the nook and disappeared.

She didn't share classes with any of the people she saw at the gathering. Part of her had been curious to hear what they had to say about it. All of the rumours were spread by those who hadn't been there.

Luckily for her, nobody had made the connection between Sam's fired shots and the wound on the side of her head. It wouldn't have surprised her if they had blamed her for Betty's disappearance if they were to find out.

She could already hear the rumours. She cut them off before they got too loud inside her mind.

The darkness spread through the whole school at a rapid pace. The teachers could not put up with it. Some even joined the children in discussing the incident, and by the time the first period was over, the board had decided to host the Talent Show early and then let the children go home.

Melody found Ford in the hall walking next to a friend. She watched them from afar, jealous of the closeness between the two boys. The playful jabs. The laughter. The looks.

She had a close friend, too, but the girl was more often absent than present at school due to some sickness that she never knew how to pronounce. Either way, it took the only connection Melody had outside of her family away from her more often than not.

She tried not to think about it.

The auditorium was hot. Air heavy with dust and old wood and the varnish of the floorboards. The folding chairs groaned beneath the weight of students pressed shoulder to shoulder as they shifted. Her brother was somewhere in the front with the rest of his year. She was further towards the back, sitting all by herself at the end of her row in her wheelchair. Teachers lined the walls with folded arms. Some looked at her. At the bandages on the side of her head. Lights hummed overhead. One flickered in the corner. The crowd's murmur was low and restless.

Melody looked down at the fabric of her dress. She smoothed it and folded her hands on top. The dress had been ironed flat, but still she felt plain and ugly. She pinched the fabric and pulled it lower to cover her lame leg. The fabric rested unevenly and caused her to shift. She winced in pain. Melody felt the press of eyes behind her though no one turned. She could hear whispers though no one spoke. Her chest was tight.

The curtain trembled. The first act walked out from behind its red wall.

A boy in oversized clothes with a harmonica. He stood stiff before the microphone. His face pale with effort. He raised the instrument and began to play. Three songs run together. The notes are thin and quavering. A faint, reedy wail that seemed to hang in the air and then fall lifeless. He finished. A few claps sounded. He bowed and left the stage.

Melody exhaled slowly. Her stomach clenched.

The second act came. A girl with long hair and a scared face. She had been there at the campfire. Melody remembered her. She stood at the microphone with her arms drawn tight. She began to sing. She was shaking, and with her, so did her voice tremble. It was a high pitch. It cracked on the top notes, and the crowd tittered. The girl's knuckles whitened where she gripped the microphone stand. It made Melody think of her own hands and the way they trembled when eyes were on her. The song ended in silence. No applause followed. Not until a teacher coughed and forced a slow clap. The others followed as the girl hurried off.

Melody shifted again. She searched the crowd for her brother but couldn't find him. Ford had told her that morning that he had planned to draw a whole comic for the show, but the teachers told him that they couldn't accept it. It sounded stupid to Melody.

She found her neck to be damp. It was as if someone was breathing down upon it. She pressed her palm over her nape and wiped away some of the beads. She inhaled and felt as though the floorboards shifted beneath her. She glanced to her right. Nothing was there except for an odd, invisible pressure drawing her in. She clutched at the wheels and held them steady, feeling them start to turn.

"No," she whispered. "Stay steady."

She then looked to her left and saw the same empty chair that had been there for her just in case she wanted to sit in it.

A boy appeared on stage, and there were claps before he even got going. It was Vince. As soon as her eyes laid on him, she forgot all about the pressure and the unevenness of the floor or even the sweat all over her back.

Vince stood by the microphone with his guitar. Tall and loose-limbed. His hair curled over his forehead. He moved with ease. The kind of ease that seemed untouchable. He slung the guitar down and waited for the claps and cheers to subside. He brushed the hair from his face with the back of his hand. The lights caught him and set his features in a sheen.

He cleared his throat as soon as there was silence. He strummed once. The chord rang out clear and true. The auditorium was his. He had them—he had Melody—at the tips of his fingers. The sound was soft at first. A slow build. Notes strung together like water falling over stone. The music filled the space and stilled the voices. His fingers moved sure and quick across the strings. He closed his eyes and sang. The voice is deep for his age.

Melody laced her fingers together and squeezed. She felt the sound press against her chest. The heat and the crowd and the ache in her leg fell away. The song lifted her. For a moment she forgot the room. She forgot the whispers and the wound and the campfire. She forgot the nightmare. She wanted to rise. To move her body to the music. She closed her eyes and let herself go into the hands of imagination. Her limbs free. Her leg straight and strong as she twirled hand in hand with the notes of the guitar.

A smile came upon her lips. She leaned forward as though to step out of her wheelchair. And then she felt it.

A shift in the air. Cold against her shoulder. The sudden press of a presence thick as smoke. She turned to her left. The empty seat was occupied. The figure was there with its body clothed in tatters. Rags hung from shoulders narrow and bent.

Melody's breath caught in her throat. She turned her eyes back to the stage. Vince played on. The crowd swayed, and she wished to sway with them. But she couldn't. The figure was there, and she was the only one to see it.

"Pretty song," the whisper invaded her mind.

She swallowed.

"I ask you, do you wish to dance?"

Her lips pressed tight.

"You want him to see you. He never looks your way."

Her chest rose hard. She stared at the boy. His curled hair fell over his eyes. His mouth against the microphone.

The figure chuckled. A dry sound.

"I ask again. Do you wish to dance? To his music, perhaps?"

She hesitated.

"I can help. I can teach you."

Her stomach knotted. She shut her eyes. The music filled her. The crowd clapped in rhythm. She could see herself rising. She could see herself spinning light across the stage and falling into Vince's arms.

"Say yes."

The last chord struck. The sound carried all the way to her and broke against her mind. The crowd roared. Students stamped their feet on the floor. Vince bowed once and caused another roar. He raised his arms and smiled. They kept him on the stage until their throats were sore and their palms ached. She wanted to be part of it.

The figure leaned in. It smelled of dust and stone and the damp of cellars.

"One last time. Do you wish to dance?"

She turned her head. She looked into the shadow beneath the hat and saw nothing. That nothing looked back.

"Yes," she said.

It was as if the darkness shifted. "How much do you wish for it?"

"With my whole heart!" she panted.

The darkness shifted once more. She blinked. The seat beside her was empty. The applause thundered on.

"Because someone must believe in you," he said. "If not him, then I."

Then he stepped back. The air around him blurred. The rags of his clothes flickered as though caught in invisible wind. For a heartbeat she thought she saw his feet hovering an inch above the ground.

When she blinked, he was gone.

She sat there a while, listening to the sound of her own breath. The night felt different now—warmer, or maybe just less lonely. She touched her shoulder and realized it no longer hurt.

She wheeled herself through the gate, up the path, and into the sleeping house. As she closed the door behind her, she whispered the names he'd spoken—Yeats, Rilke, Lorca—like a charm, as if repeating them might keep the world from closing in.

In her room, she sat by the window and looked at the sky. The moon had climbed higher, framed by a faint halo of clouds. Somewhere beneath it, she thought, the Eggstabletman was walking; soft, careful steps along some other road, teaching another lost soul how to move again.

She didn't know if that thought comforted her or frightened her.

Before she slept, she wrote one line in her notebook:

If he doesn't see me, the fault is in his eyes, not my light.

2

CHANGES

The tent was vast and empty. The coloured canvas above sagged with age. The air smelled of straw and smoke. The lamps burned low along the stage.

Melody's chair stood alone at the edge of the boards. She sat with her hands folded in her lap. The sound was gone altogether.

The curtains parted, and he appeared. The Eggstabletman.

He stepped into the light. Flame wicks licked the walls of the tent and the edges of the giant-eggs, but his shadow did not stretch. He disappeared behind one of the eggs. Reappeared again. Much closer. She tried to turn in order to leave, but her body was paralyzed. His burning red eyes dripped down into the shadows of his face. His long nails scraped as he walked.

He stopped before her. He bowed his head.

"Rise."

Melody stared at him.

"Rise," he repeated.

He bent low. His long fingers slid beneath her arm. Cold as stone. He lifted. She felt her legs tremble. She felt weight where there had only been weakness.

She stood.

"See?"

She swayed. She did not fall. She felt her body held upright in this amber air around her. Her legs steadied beneath her. Whole. Yet she could not move them. Not a single part.

He stepped back. Took her hand. The nails curved black against her skin. He raised her arm and led her onto the stage. The boards creaked. Around them lay the vast pale shapes of the eggs. She only caught glimpses of them. She dared not look too long, feeling their emptiness.

The Eggstabletman pulled her forward. He turned her once in a slow circle. Her dress swung at her knees. Her legs moved sure beneath her on their own. They passed one egg, then another. He led her between them. His bare feet are dragging. His hat shadowing his glowing eyes.

"You can dance, you see," he whispered.

Her chest swelled. She felt her heart beat hard. Her body carried with it the lightness of hope that had dimmed out of her so long ago she had forgotten about it. He turned her, and she did not stumble. The boards were firm beneath her. He guided her. Step by step. The music of a strange guitar from a world away, a world so far and so familiar, rang in her ears. She thought for a moment she might lift from the floor and vanish into the air.

He stopped. "You are mine."

Melody desperately wanted to shake her head. But she couldn't. He raised her hand again and turned her slowly. The eggs circled them. Cracks began to form. There were faces in the dark of them. Eyes dull and watching. Crying. He pressed her closer.

"You *will* dance."

Her eyes filled with tears.

"You wish for it, don't you?"

Melody felt her lips move against her will. "Yes," she said.

The Eggstabletman vanished. She stood centre-stage on her own, surrounded by the giant eggs. Their shells cracked further and further and then snapped. A darkness spilled out from within. One that reached for her. Before she could feel its touch, Melody woke with a cry.

It hadn't been loud enough. Nobody heard her.

Her room was dark and still. The moon stretched across the ceiling. She inhaled and felt the smell of dust still in her nose. She closed her eyes and fell into a dreamless sleep.

The morning after her second nightmare, she spoke nothing of it. A passing glance from India led the woman to suspect that something might be wrong with her daughter, but she said nothing of it until Victor was out on the farm to work the land.

"So," she cleared her throat. Ford moved to the living room to draw. He left behind a sketch of Melody in her wheelchair dressed in knight's armor. "What's on your mind, Mel?"

"Nothing." She held the drawing close and looked at it. "Why?"

"Something's pressing on you, sweetie. You don't have to hide it from me."

"Nothing's wrong. I'm telling you."

India took the empty plates and moved them to the sink. She turned on the tap to rinse them and popped them in the dishwasher. "If it has to do with your birthday, I'm sorry, honey. We just don't have the money right now."

Melody dropped her spoon in her bowl of cereal and turned to her mother. "It's not that," she said. "I forgot all about it. It's today, isn't it?"

"We'll make up for it."

"You don't have to. It's alright."

India rolled her eyes. She came to the table and drew a chair close. "Don't say that to me. I know what that means, okay? I don't want you to think that we don't love you."

"Well—"

"Please, honey. It's hard. We're scared. Your father's working himself harder than ever. I am taking extra shifts, too, just to pay the bills. We're trying."

"Mom, I know. It's fine. I'm not stupid. I told you I forgot about it anyway. I had no expectations."

India took her daughter's hands in her own. She brushed her fingers gently with her thumb. Tears welled up in her eyes.

"It's just so hard with Baller gone and working away at college. When he was here, he helped your father so much, and with him gone, there's hardly anything we can do. I help, and Ford does too but—" She stopped. She inhaled deeply and wiped away her tears. "Look at me. What am I doing? I'm such a child sometimes. I'm sorry, honey. I guess things just piled up."

India stood up and turned from her daughter instantly. She paced towards the kitchen counter and found some tissue to blow her nose in.

"Mom?"

"Mhmm?"

"It doesn't matter to me if we're poor or not. I'll still love you and Dad."

India said nothing. She just left the room in a hurry. A while later, when Melody was done with her breakfast and cleaned up after herself, she heard her mother sobbing in her room. She stood by the door, tempted to go in, but she didn't. She just listened to parts inside of her dislodging and coming undone.

Victor worked the field that whole day and only came in when it was dark. She had not seen him but heard him as he stumbled through the kitchen looking for food. She was in the bathroom brushing her teeth.

Melody wondered what it was that went on inside her father's head. He was the most hard-working person she knew, even though he never once felt happy about it. His words always came out light in a way that felt as if somebody else had said them first and he just repeated what he'd heard.

Not once did he feel any malice coming from him, only concern that went a little too far.

She wheeled herself out of the bathroom. She lingered in the hall for a moment, watching the faint yellow light coming out of the kitchen. The sound of his existence was quiet and clumsy. It was, in its own way, comforting.

Before going into her room, she passed by Ford's.

She found him sketching away in bed. "What are you working on?"

"A monster."

"Gave up on heroes already?"

Ford shook his head. "At night I sketch the monsters. Daytime is for heroes that beat them."

"What monster are you working on now? Can I see?" Ford looked up from his drawing pad. "No."

"What? Why not?"

Ford shook his head. "You're not allowed."

"Fordie...you always show me what you draw."

"Not this one. Maybe I'll show you once I'm done. I'm not allowed to until then."

"Who's not letting you?"

"You're asking too many questions Mel. It's all mysterious and spooky stuff. You wouldn't get it. You're a girl."

"Hey!"

"Sorry," he lowered his head. "But it's true."

"You'd be surprised. Good night now. Don't stay up too late now, okay?"

"Okay."

She wheeled herself into her room and instantly knew she wasn't alone. She turned on the light and saw him. He sat in the far corner of the room at the dimmest point of light.

Melody closed the door.

"Dance," the whisper said.

For a while she sat and watched. He seemed more patient than ever. Or perhaps time had slowed down. As her gaze lingered, she found that she did not think of the fear she felt on seeing him in her dreams. All she thought of was the dance they shared not long ago.

"You wish for it to happen here. It can."

She wheeled herself close to the wall. She used it as leverage to prop herself up. He came and pulled the chair away from her.

"Hey, no!" she cried.

"You don't need it."

In the mirror she saw only herself. Thin arms. Hair falling across her face. Yet he was behind her. His shadow bent low. The brim of his hat drawn over his face.

"Spin," he said.

She did as she was told. Or at least, she tried. Her foot dragged. She grimaced.

"Spin."

She raised her arms as he showed her. She bent the knee. She lifted her chin. She tried to take the step.

"Come on."

She faltered. She caught the dresser with her hand. Her breath ragged.

"Do it," he said. "You can."

She nodded and tried again.

The days stretched. The nights deepened. He came when the house was quiet. She felt his breath in her ear as though they were words that were not meant to be heard. Not even by her. Her body ached day and night as she followed his rhythm. Muscles long unused screamed against her. She pressed on despite the pain.

At breakfast, her father looked at her hands. The knuckles raw from gripping the chair.

"Practicing again?" he said chewing. His mind was distracted.

Melody nodded.

"Good girl," he smiled. He looked at India. "Isn't she good, honey?"

The mother's lips parted, but the words were a silent rush of air saying nothing.

"Isn't she?" Victor asked again and thumped her shin with his foot.

"O-of course. I just worry that you might be straining yourself, Mel."

"A good bit of effort never hurts anybody, India," the father nodded with pride. "I'll tell you that much. I've been breaking my back on the farm ever since I was a twerp. Smaller than Ford here. And look at me. I'm still going, ain't I?"

"You always complain about your back, Pap," Ford said.

Victor regarded his son for a moment. "Give the boy some more food, India. His mouth's too empty."

Melody watched them in silence, eating quickly, her mind on nothing but her room and the dark figure awaiting in the corner.

Weeks passed. She moved into her room with the curtains drawn. She raised her arms. She stepped and turned. Her dress hem swung at her knees. Her breath was sharp in her chest.

He circled her. Soft voice guiding.

"Lift. Higher. Again."

Her body strained. Sweat dark on her dress. She stumbled and fell but did not stop. She rose again and went. She ignored the sound of footsteps stopping at her door. She could tell that her parents listened in on her but it didn't matter. As much as they wanted to step in she wasn't going to let them.

"Mel?" her mother called. Melody ignored her. "Mel, honey. Can we talk?"

Nothing.

"Do you mind if I come in?"

"Please don't," she finally said. "Not now."

"But later?"

"Maybe."

"Okay, honey. Just be careful, please."

"I *am*."

Her mother retreated in silence.

Autumn came. The leaves burned red and gold. The air cooled down and left behind the summer. The girl's body thinned. Her cheeks hollow. She moved still. Night after night. Her breath rasping in her throat. Her legs quivering under her.

Her mother no longer stood in the hall listening. She didn't bring up the dancing at the dinner table either. She did look, though, with concern upon her daughter. She understood what it meant for a child to need an activity. For a child to want to progress in life despite their condition. But to see her own daughter struggle so much. To see the effect it had on her body. It was hard to accept.

She lay on the sofa staring at the ceiling. Pots bubbled in the kitchen, filling the house with the rich smell of food, although the windows were all open to try and expel it. India didn't want the scent to cling to the furniture.

Her mother's phone rang for a while. Ford was with his father outside. The cold had not set in fully. They were preparing the land for its long winter slumber.

"Mel, honey?"

"Yes?" She turned her head. Her mother held her phone to her chest and smiled.

"Can he?"

Melody shook her head. "I don't want to talk to him."

India sighed. "She doesn't want to, Ball. That's what you get. No. She won't. I'm telling you she won't. Why are you putting me in a situation like this? It's enough that—Okay. Fine. Here," she paced to the edge of the sofa. "Honey. I'm sorry. He's insisting."

The mother placed the phone to Melody's ear and held it.

"Hello? Melody? Are you there? Can you hear me?" Baller's voice sounded the same as ever. She had been certain that it was going to be that way. That was part of the reason she didn't want to speak with him. How could he skip out—not only on Thanksgiving and Christmas, but her birthday, too? She had turned 15 this summer, and he had not been there. He hadn't even sent her a gift. "Come on, girl. Don't be cross with me. I know I messed up, alright? Life carried me away. I got picked up and didn't think to look left and right. I met me a girl here. Her name's Lorena. She's very nice. You'd love her. I'm gonna bring her when I visit. Don't know if Pap's gonna like her. But let's leave me out of this for a second. What's this I'm hearing about dancing? You got yourself on the move?"

"How do you know?"

Baller hesitated. He didn't expect the girl to speak. "Mom told me."

"Right."

"She do bad?"

Melody said nothing.

"Well, if she did bad then I don't know nothing about no dancing. It's nice, though."

"You think?" She tried not to smile.

"You bet. It'd do you good I'd say, if you were to pick it up."

She played with her lean fingers in silence. "Some people don't think so."

"Whys that? They think you'd work yourself too hard?"

"Exactly."

"Would you work yourself too hard?"

She hesitated. "Maybe. But I'd like it," she said.

"All that matters."

"Baller?"

"Yes?"

"When are you coming back home?"

She did not like the silence that followed.

"That's a hard one, sprout."

"Don't call me that."

"You like being called that," he said.

"Not anymore."

"Well, alright. My bad. I—"

Melody craned her head away from the phone. "I don't want it any-more," she said to her mother.

India pursed her lips and took back the phone. "Hey, Ball? It's me. Yeah, she's done." She lingered a while longer, watching her daughter as she closed her eyes and then left back into the kitchen. "Ford's outside. He's been asking about you. What are you getting up to over there, Ball? What are you hiding? You're not getting into any crazy research, are you? Have you heard? Another one went missing. Well..."

Winter came without Baller. It didn't matter. Melody moved. She was slower. Exhausted. Still, she rose each day and night and practiced. She learned to do so when the house was most silent. When only Ford was indoors. He did not come to disturb her.

The Eggstabletman clung to the walls of the room like smoke. At times he moved with her. Mostly he watched.

"Again," he'd whisper.

She still stumbled. She fell to her knees often. She gasped and cried. He would bend low and lift her up. "Again," he'd say.

She wept but obeyed all the same. She rose and moved. Her breath ragged. Her body wrung dry.

In the mornings she came to breakfast pale as chalk. Victor no longer talked about it. He looked as worried as her mother. India's glances shifted cautiously.

"What are you working on there, Fordie?" Melody asked in a frail voice.

"On a new Super-Mel!" the little brother said. "This one's a dancer."

She smiled and looked up at her parents. Their gazes forced her to stare into her bowl and continue eating in silence.

Nothing more was said.

By spring, her movements had grown smooth. Her leg carried her where it had not before. Her body obeyed. She lifted her arms and turned. She spun once and did not fall.

She stopped. Breathless. A smile blessed her lips.

The figure leaned near. "See?"

She nodded.

"You wished with all your heart, and I made it happen. What now? What is your wish?"

The figure disappeared before Melody could answer.

Towards the back-end of 2015's spring, the school held another Talent Show. The corridors by then were no longer filled with whispers of Betty. At least not of her disappearance. Some spoke of the places she might have ended up in. The things she might have done. Melody didn't think of the girl at all. She had no time. She had spent a whole year learning how to dance. She still needed her wheelchair to move around.

She told no one of her participation. Not even her brother. Word travelled, though. Teachers spoke to one another, and the nosy children heard that she might have an act ready for the show. No one took it seriously. They all thought it a joke. But it wasn't.

The auditorium was full. The smell of dust mingled with the hot sweat clinging to bodies. Lights buzzed overhead. Students pressed close and shifted on their folding chairs.

Melody sat stiff in her seat near the back. She kept her eyes fixed on the stage, though she saw little. Her chest rose shallow.

Names were called. One act and then another. A boy with a trumpet. A girl who juggled bright scarves. Applause rising and falling with each breath. She heard none of it. Her name waited on the sheet. She felt it press around the edges of her mind. Her eyes scanned the crowd. Not for her brother. Not for Vince.

For the Eggstabletman. She couldn't find him.

At last, her name was called. *Melody Sook.*

A ripple moved through the room. They turned and found her and were all silent.

"Mel?!" Ford stood up, a smile on his face. "You're doing this?!"

She wheeled herself to the front of the crowd. She spared only a faint smile for her brother. It was all that he needed. He squealed excitedly and sat down, his eyes on her.

"Do you need help?" A teacher came to her side as soon as she reached the three steps leading up onto the stage.

"No," she said.

"Are you sure? It'll be quick."

"I'm sure."

The walk-up was as much a part of her routine as the dance she had prepared. A deep breath. She pushed up against the chair. Her dress straightened. It took her a while to steady herself. She felt each gaze pressing tightly against her.

She took her first step, then her second, and then she was up on the stage. She turned towards her brother. He had his fingers in his mouth and chewed on them. His eyes wide.

A deep breath. She paced to centre stage. She was stable. Steady. Straight. She was walking. Typically, her energy drained rather quickly with such a display, but her heart beat too rapidly for her to feel fatigued.

Once centre-stage, she turned. The light hit her. Hot and white. The faces before her blurred in the dark. A sea of strange eyes that had looked at her for years and always saw nothing. Not anymore.

The music began. Melody raised her arms.

The first step faltered. The leg is slow to follow. She almost stumbled. She caught herself. Her arms still lifted. She bent and swayed. The music carried her forward. She turned. Her balance was wavering. Her foot dragged across the creaking boards. She pressed on. Eyes closed.

The crowd was silent. She felt them watching. A hundred stares heavy on her. She felt her heart pounding in her throat. She moved again. She lifted her chin like she was taught. Like she learned. She reached with her arms the way he had shown her. Her breath came ragged. Her body strained. Still, she turned.

The hem of her dress swung about her knees. The air it created was the only coolness she felt. The lights burned like a dozen suns. The boards thumped beneath her steps. She heard the faint laughter of someone near the back. Then came her brother's *hush*. She kept on. She kept her eyes closed.

She bent low and rose again. Her arms spread wide. Her chest opened. For a moment the music seemed to lift her. The pain fell away. She turned again and opened her eyes.

She saw him clinging to the ceiling. Upside down. Its tattered clothes did not obey the laws of the world. Its long claws dug into the boards and held him there, upside down. He watched her. Her breath caught for a moment. She stumbled. He shook his head and watched her recover.

The song swelled, and she gave herself to it. She let the steps come as they would. Awkward. Sluggish. Yet hers. Each movement wrung from her body. Each motion was a victory over the limb that betrayed her in the womb 15 years prior.

Her arms rose high. She turned once more. She held the pose. Her body was shaking with effort. She stretched higher as though to reach for the lights. To feel the warmth of the many suns in her palms and to draw it close inside herself. To cast away his darkness.

The music ended. Silence. Total and thick.

"YES!" Ford jumped and punched the air. "YES MEL! LET'S GOOO!"

He started clapping. Others joined in. He was the loudest, but the others weren't bad either. They were real. A scattering of them. A whistle. A shout, maybe. Her cheeks burned. She bowed and turned to walk to the edge of the stage. There she froze.

He was there waiting. Not the Eggstabletman but Vince. His guitar slung over his shoulder. He looked up at her with a smile on his face. He had to shake the curls away from his eyes.

"Cool," he said.

"You think?"

"Super cool," he nodded. "Need help?"

"Well—"

She could feel herself already shaking. She took the first step down on her own. She tried for the second, too, but her foot slipped and she fell forward.

"Easy!" He swung the guitar onto his back and lunged to catch her just in time. "You good?"

She felt something she never thought would be possible. His arms were around her, holding her close. She could smell him. She didn't know what the scent was, but she remembered dreaming of it once. A bright dream. A good dream. One before all the horrors.

"I'm good."

"I've got to get up on stage now. See you after?"

"After?" She sat down. "Like after school?"

"Sure."

Melody nodded. She watched him get up on stage and wave at the crowd. They cheered for him and in their screams and claps she drowned and became forgotten.

She waited for him after school, but Vince never showed. The last bus came and went and left her behind with no one to help her. Melody turned and started to wheel herself home. The street-lights hummed. A sound that oddly blurred the edges of her mind enough for her to see past its restraints. To trace back the memory of the auditorium. His face and smile and promise. All for nothing.

The sidewalk glistened from earlier rain. Her arms already ached from the performance and the waiting. Each push of the wheels made her shoulders burn. The world around her was quiet. Only the wet whisper of tires on distant pavement and the rhythm of her own motion.

After a while, the air behind her shifted. It wasn't a sound at first, but a weight, a feeling of being watched in the most neutral way possible. She slowed the chair.

From the corner of her vision, something darker than the night moved beside her. The Eggstabletman.

He walked at her pace, short and small in stature, the brim of his hat cutting his face from the streetlight. He said nothing for a long time. The only sound was the low squeak of her wheels and the whisper of cloth brushing his knees.

When he finally spoke, his voice was softer than she remembered.

"Let me."

The chair moved though her hands had stopped. The wheels turned as if pushed by invisible palms. The motion was smooth, effortless, like sliding over water.

"You looked lovely tonight," he said. "Even the lights liked you."

She stared ahead. "Why are you saying that?"

"Because I mean it."

Melody hesitated. "I missed my bus," she said.

"I know."

He guided the chair around a puddle. The reflection of the lamp post shimmered in it, long and trembling. He did not show through.

Her arms relaxed for the first time that night. The pain in her shoulders began to fade. Warmth flowed through her, slow and deliberate, as if the air itself were smoothing her bones.

"Why are you helping me?"

"Silly question," he said. "I helped you before. I taught you how to dance."

He had not lied. Yet she had never thought about it in that way. He was a creature too dark for her to associate her dancing capabilities with him, even if he was right.

The road stretched before them, empty, quiet, framed by hedges heavy with rain.

After a while he said, "You wanted him to come, didn't you? Vince."

She hesitated, then nodded her head.

"A boy like that hears too many sounds at once, Melody. Music, words, the noise of other people. You are a quiet girl. It'll be hard for him to hear you. If you try to make noise, it will never break through. What you need to give him is what you're best at. Silence.

She smiled faintly. "That's oddly poetic."

"Good. I've read plenty." His tone was light, almost amused. "Would you like me to teach you some?"

She looked up at him, surprised. "Teach me?"

He tilted his head. "You want him to notice you. He loves words, yes? And music. Those things can also be silent. Captivating. They don't have to be just noise. I can show you."

Something in his voice made the night feel smaller, like a world had folded in around them.

"All right," she said. "Teach me."

He began to speak names.

"Yeats, Rilke, Lorca," he said, each one like a note plucked from air. "Listen to their rhythm, not their meaning. Poetry is a kind of heartbeat. People forget that."

He told her about the intervals of music—the perfect fifth, the minor second—and how they lived in the spaces between motions. "If you can talk about them," he said, "you can make any musician listen."

His words came like soft rain, steady and hypnotic. She imagined herself telling these things to Vince, the way he might look at her with surprise, maybe admiration.

"But I won't see him again," she said. "He'll move on. I'll move on. This was just something small. It'll fade."

The Eggstabletman shook his head. "Then it doesn't matter. If he doesn't see your worth, he's unworthy of seeing at all."

Melody wanted to believe him.

They passed under the long stretch of oaks near the park. The streetlights thinned. The night deepened until the air felt almost liquid. She could hear the faint pulse of frogs near the creek.

"You carry too much doubt," he said. "That limp of yours, it's in your heart, too, not just your leg."

"It's not something I can fix."

"Everything can be fixed if you stop believing it's broken."

She didn't answer. The wind stirred the branches overhead, scattering droplets that flashed silver before they fell.

He continued, voice steady. "There was a dancer once," he said. "She couldn't move her left arm. She came to me and said she wanted to be whole. I told her to stop wanting. Just move. Wholeness follows motion."

"Did it work?"

"For a while."

His tone held no sadness, only certainty.

They reached the edge of her neighbourhood. The houses stood dark, sleeping. He slowed the chair as they turned onto her street. She realized her limbs felt light, her breathing even. The pain in her body was gone, replaced by a calm that felt borrowed.

When they reached her gate, he stopped. The moon had risen pale above the roofs, lighting the path in faint silver.

He leaned down until his voice was level with her ear.

"Remember what I said tonight. Read. Listen. Learn to speak the language of what you love."

She looked up at him. "Why are you doing this?"

"Because someone must believe in you," he said. "If not him, then I."

Then he stepped back. The air around him blurred. The rags of his clothes flickered as though caught in invisible wind. For a heartbeat she thought she saw his feet hovering an inch above the ground.

When she blinked, he was gone.

She sat there a while, listening to the sound of her own breath. The night felt different now—warmer, or maybe just less lonely. She touched her shoulder and realized it no longer hurt.

She wheeled herself through the gate, up the path, and into the sleeping house. As she closed the door behind her, she whispered the names he'd spoken—Yeats, Rilke, Lorca—like a charm, as if repeating them might keep the world from closing in.

In her room, she sat by the window and looked at the sky. The moon had climbed higher, framed by a faint halo of clouds. Somewhere beneath it, she thought, the Eggstabletman was walking; soft, careful steps along some other road, teaching another lost soul how to move again.

She didn't know if that thought comforted her or frightened her.

Before she slept, she wrote one line in her notebook:

If he doesn't see me, the fault is in his eyes, not my light.

3

Thanksgiving

The tent stood silent in the dark. The lamps above burned faintly. The canvas sagged with age. The seats were empty.

She stood on the diving board high above the ring. The plank narrows beneath her feet. The air is dry and close. She swayed once and steadied herself.

Below lay the pool. Wide as the ring itself. Black and still. The light from above shone on it in strange reflection. Not water. The glints of light made the black surface red as wine. Only for a moment. The pool stretched smooth and perfect. Still as death itself. A mirror. She saw herself from far away. Pale and small upon it.

The smell of iron rose sharp.

She looked out across the tent. The stands are dark and silent. Shapes there like ghosts floating in and out of the tent. The sound of her own breath filled her ears.

Behind her came a weight upon the board. It shifted. The wood creaked. A presence cold at her back. The brim of a hat. The whisper of rags.

"My girl," he said.

Melody did not respond.

"Look down," he whispered. "Look down at what's to come."

She held still. She had looked before but now she did not want to. She feared what she might see. Melody could not resist the figure's will. It pressed against her and forced the girl to do his bidding.

The pool waited below. Its surface is unbroken. The reflection of the lamps shivered in it. She felt the height rise up in her stomach. She felt her body light with dread.

The board lurched. Melody fell.

The air tore past her. The lamps wheeled overhead. The seats spun. The pool rushed upward.

She struck.

The blood broke open and closed again. The sound is hollow and final. She sank.

The liquid was thick around her. Slow and heavy. It filled her ears. It pressed against her eyes. Her body moved sluggish as if bound. She flailed once and sank deeper.

The pool was endless. No bottom. Only the weight dragging her down. The light above grew faint. Her reflection is gone.

Shapes stirred in the depths. Pale-skinned limbs in the dark coming to get her. Bodies curled in silence. Eyes dim and open. Their hair is floating like weeds. She sank among them.

Her lungs burned. Her throat opened. The blood pressed into her mouth. Bitter and hot. Her arms reached upward. Her fingers spread. The surface was gone. Only blackness.

Melody drifted down. The bodies parted to make room. Their mouths moved soundless. Their faces pale as if from another world, peering through.

She felt her chest shudder. She felt her body give. The blood filled her and she stilled.

The pool held her. Her eyes wide. Her hair spread about her like smoke. The tent above is gone. The lamps are gone. The seats are gone. Only the red and the black and the silence.

And death.

There among the shadows he stood. Far below the surface. Hat low. Rags billowing in the sea of blood. His shape still. His arms open.

She sank toward him. The last air left her lips in a stream of bubbles that burst and vanished. Her body fell, deeper and deeper. The pool closed above.

And all was dark.

The house smelled of flour and onions. The clatter of pans. India bent over the counter with sleeves rolled back, her hands dusted white. She moved slowly, steadily. Victor came in with boots caked in soil. He left them by the door. His shoulders bent from the cold.

Tomorrow was the day.

Melody sat at the kitchen table. Her elbows drawn in. She turned the pages of a book she did not read. Her hair hung about her face. The lamplight lay pale across her cheekbones. Ford sat opposite. His sketchbook is open. The sound of pencil scratching. He looked at her in quick glances, then back to the page.

The room warmed from the oven. Steam rising from pots. The window glass fogged.

"We need more firewood for the stove," said Victor. He rubbed his hands before the heat. "I'll go bring some."

Melody watched her father retreat into his own world. The outside, somehow, belonged to him alone. There was nobody else that could claim it, not when he spent so much time toiling away at it.

He returned not long after, his boots still on his feet as he carried an armful of logs.

"Don't track mud all over the place now. I just cleaned," India warned him.

Melody raised her eyes once and let them fall again, as though she feared that she might see something she did not want to if she kept them up too long.

Ford turned his book. A figure on the page. His sister was standing tall. Her arms spread. Around her, shadows drawn in broad strokes. He smiled.

"What do you think?" he asked.

"What is it?"

"You," he said.

"I know that. I meant the shadows. What are they?"

Ford took his sketch back. He looked at it. Then back at her. "I dunno," he shrugged. "It's just you, Mel. That's all it is."

Melody looked over her shoulder. She saw nothing there but the backdrop of her house.

The hours slipped. The kitchen is filled with dishes waiting to be baked or set aside. Jars of cranberries. Loaves of bread rising. India's face is lined with weariness.

Victor brought in a basket of squash. He laid it on the counter. He kissed India on the forehead and went out again. Melody wondered how long he could go on like that for. How long could all of it continue in the same manner before it snapped and broke loose. Who would it be that would go first? That would realize something was wrong. It was not present day today. Not layered over the surface of things. But buried deep. So deep that it could not be seen or felt or anything of that manner.

Melody sat still. Her hand resting on the cover of the book she had not touched. India looked at her.

"You're quiet today, Mel," she said.

"Not really."

"You tired?"

"A little," she nodded.

"How's your dancing going?"

Melody shrugged. "I haven't danced in a while."

The girl's room was cold. Curtains drawn tight. She had left the crutch she now carried against the dresser. In the corner the shadows lengthened. She stood there long after the lamp was out.

Her dreams came heavy each night. The tent. The pool. The voice beneath the hat. She woke with her body stiff, her mouth dry, her eyes hollow.

She told no one.

At the table each day she smiled faintly when spoken to. She gave short answers. She ate little. The parents mistook her silence for peace. They were grateful the storms had stilled. They did not see how the shadows clung to her.

At school she grew distant from the world. A pity. People were finally starting to see her. The performance she gave last year. Vince's smile. It all contributed toward an attempt at bringing her back into the world. Yet she could not pass through the threshold. The Eggstabletman's presence held her still. He was the one who had opened the door for her. Showed her the way to the other side. When it came time to step through, he held her in place. Not letting her go. As if to tease her with what could be.

Ford watched Melody more than the rest. He drew her in new shapes. Her face blurred with shading. Her arms outstretched. Sometimes her eyes ringed dark. Sometimes flames behind her.

He followed her at school and saw her linger around a group of recluses. Those deeper in the dark than she had ever been. A cult-like presence loomed over those kids. Ford didn't understand what his sister saw in them, and neither did he dare get close enough to find out. Instead, he drew. More and more of Melody. There were pages that he kept hidden under his bed. He showed her none of those.

The evenings stretched on long. Preparations for Thanksgiving. Sounds of knives chopping. The low music of the radio. The wind outside rattled the windows. Victor came in from the cold. He sat at the table and drank his coffee.

"What's that there?" He took a look at one of Ford's drawings, "That your sister?"

Ford nodded.

"Who's that man behind her? The one with the brimmed hat?"

Melody looked up. Ford glanced at her. He said nothing.

"Alright buddy," Victor smiled and passed the page back. "Keep your secrets. I was never meant to understand the mind of an artist anyway. The field's for me. Let's see." He took a long sip from his mug. His hands laced around it as he set it back down on the table. "School going good, you two?"

Melody and Ford nodded together. "Good," he smiled. "That's good."

"Wanna help with the pies, darling?"

"Me?" Victor stood." No, no. I've still got work to do outside. Maybe Melody. " He smiled. "What do you say?"

"Victor!"

"Let her be. She can do it. Can't you, Mel? You've got it."

"Sure..." she muttered and stood up. It took her a little while to stabilize. But she managed.

She got to work right away, right next to her mother. They pressed the flour into the dough. Her movements are careful. Her hands pale against the white. She looked older in the lamplight.

India glanced at her from time to time. She felt the weight of something in the room, but she pushed it aside.

Thanksgiving was a day away.

Night fell hard. The fields are dark. The barns are silent. The sky without stars.

The family gathered in the living room. Victor with the newspaper. India with her knitting. Ford, as always, sketching away.

Melody sat apart. The firelight flickered against her face. Her eyes half closed. Her mind elsewhere. Victor said something about the weather holding up tomorrow. "Clear skies," he said.

"It will be good to be all together for once," India smiled.

"Except we're not," Melody retorted. They turned to her. "Baller isn't here. He's never here anymore."

India turned to Victor. She didn't know what to say.

"Your brother's busy," Victor sighed. "He needs to put his life together. He's at that stage. Nothing we can do, sweetie. We have to give him time. He'll come back eventually."

"By then I'll be gone," she said. "I'll be gone, too. There'll only be Ford. I'll never see Baller again."

"Where'll you be gone?" India asked. "What are you talking about?"

Melody hesitated. "College," she said, shyly. "I'll be gone to college."

"Oh..."

"What?"

"N-nothing," India returned to her knitting. "That's great. That you want to go, I mean."

Melody thought of it no more. Ford drew the fire. Then he drew the figure he saw in the flames. Hat low. Ragged. Watching. He shut the book quickly when his sister looked.

Later the house grew quiet. Dishes cleaned. Lights dimmed.

The girl lay in her bed. Her body is still. Her eyes open to the dark. She listened to the wind. Against the siding. She felt the weight in the room. The clump of rags in the corner. The faint scrape of long nails.

She turned her face into the pillow. She did not sleep.

Morning would bring Thanksgiving. Hopefully, some respite along with it.

The knock came at the door late. Victor rose to answer. India wiped her hands on her apron and waited. Ford looked up.

"My boy!" Victor gasped and stepped away from sight. His words choked up.

Not much later, a figure stepped in from the cold. Baller stood there. Tall and broad. His coat buttoned. His face was red with wind. For a moment no one spoke.

"What's the matter with y'all?" he asked. "Cat got your tongues?"

Melody's eyes widened.

"You're here," she said. She bounced up out of her chair and ran to him. She stumbled and almost fell. He watched her. "You came!"

"Of course I did. I said I would. "He embraced her. "Look at you, walking on your own. How much has changed."

Ford didn't want to be left out. He leapt up and ran to him. India sobbed silently to herself, hand pressed over her mouth.

It didn't take long for the table to be fixed. An extra plate was added. The bird was carved. Bowls of squash and beans and potatoes. The bread laid in baskets. The smell of butter and sage was heavy in the room.

They all sat huddled together, as if afraid to move apart. Then Victor lowered his head in a moment of prayer. All followed suit in that solemn silence. Yet it was hard to. The atmosphere was giddy. Too giddy to be able to keep it down.

"I missed the fields," Baller said once they could speak. "California's all stone and glass. Traffic everywhere."

"Is it?"

"I dream sometimes of the rows stretching on and on, Pops," he smiled.

Victor looked at him. "You'll come back eventually. There's always a place here."

Baller smiled. He turned to India. "How's work?"

"The children keep me busy. There's this poor boy that cries each morning until his mother comes back. I carry him in my arms and sing to him and calm him down at times."

"You always knew how to handle children."

India's laugh was soft. Her eyes drew towards Melody and that softness turned into something dark and regretful. "Let's eat," she said, awkwardly, as if it had not already happened. "You've grown thin. They don't feed you over there?"

"They feed me, sure. But the food at the dorm is nothing like this."

The conversation trailed on. He asked Ford about his drawings. Ford shrugged, trying to play it cool in front of his brother. Said he drew what came to him and nothing else. Said he drew Melody the most.

"Can I see one now?"

Ford shook his head.

"Alright." He reached across the table and ruffled his hair. Ford grinned despite himself. "And school?" He turned to Melody. "Doing well?"

Melody nodded.

"What about you?" India chimed in. "What about your classes?"

Baller leaned back in his chair. "Hard but good," he said. "Studying a good bunch. The professors are strange. Some brilliant, some half asleep. I think it's the city. There's something about it. Don't let people be all the way there."

"You better not fall into that. It would be a shame." Victor pointed his fork at him.

"I know, Pops."

The meal wore on. Baller asked each of them something. He pulled them in. He looked to his father and asked about the crops, the new tractor, the fences along the south field. He looked to his mother and talked of the women in town, who had married and who had moved. He looked to Ford and asked what he wanted to be, what he dreamed of. As if he'd forgotten.

"Maybe an artist," Ford said.

"Of course."

He looked at Melody often but didn't ask her anything. He only smiled.

The plates emptied. Victor leaned back in his chair. He wiped his mouth with the cloth. India rose to fetch the pies. Baller helped her. He stood and took the plates from the table, too. Carried them to the counter. Victor watched him with quiet pride. The sweet smell of pies filled the air. India cut and served and they ate again, slowly, as the fire popped in the stove. The night pressed dark at the windows. Baller spoke low now. He said he'd come home at Christmas, too, if he could. That he didn't like being gone so long. Most believed him. Not Melody. She saw that look on his face. The lingering hesitation. But she pretended. She did because he was there for the time being. With him, the shadows seemed a little further away.

The following morning, he was already on his way. Only Victor was there to see him off. He had not told anybody.

"You sure you can't stay a little longer?" his father asked.

"Nah." Baller stared off into the distance, as though he could see into another world. "The city's calling me."

"Don't fall too in love with it, son."

"I know."

"Your mother'll be upset."

"It's not her I'm worried about, Pops." Baller turned to look at his father.

"You ain't helping," his father sighed. "The way you're coming-and-going. Melody needs you. Ford, too."

"I need me too," Baller said.

"Son." Victor squeezed his shoulder, "I know. But that's the way things are. Listen, you don't worry about a damn thing, alright? I'll take care of things here. You call. Call often. More often than you already do."

"Alright."

"Are you sure you don't need a ride?"

Baller shook his head. "You make sure Melody takes this well."

"As well as she can," Victor said.

He watched his son walk off. The shape of a young man pressed against the ice-blue horizon. He did not turn back, not even once. He just walked on, further away from home, until none of him was left.

4

CONFRONTATION

The room was dark, though in the dream it stretched wider than it ever had, the ceiling higher and the corners lost in shadow. Melody lay on her bed and felt the sheets cold against her skin. Her body was heavy and unwilling to rise. She tried to call out, but no sound came. Her voice was stilled in her throat.

From the corner came the scrape of nails. The sound she has heard one too many times now. Somehow it grew deeper, and more haunted each time. The figure emerged out of the dark. He carried nothing in his hands, but behind him trailed shapes that shuffled forward on stiff legs.

They were her family.

Victor was first: tall and broad and made of wood, his eyes glassy and dead. He moved with a stilted gait, jerking forward as if pulled by strings. The Eggstabletman guided him to the center of the room and set him there.

India followed, her hands painted white and her hair a wig of coarse fibers. Her mouth was drawn in a line of red paint, her face lifeless. Then came Ford, small and crooked at the shoulders, his hands clutching a blank book. Last of all was Baller, tall like the father, his head tipped to the side as if broken at the neck.

They stood before her in a line, mannequins posed in mockery of her family, and the Eggstabletman circled them with a gait slow and patient, his shadows stretching long across the floor.

One by one, he began to ruin them.

Victor's chest split open with a groan of wood, and inside was not sawdust but blood, dark and thick, spilling down his painted frame to the floorboards. The smell of iron filled the room. The Eggstabletman pressed his long fingers into the wound and pulled at the entrails, winding coils of wood gushing with a dark ichor. The figure collapsed.

He tore India's head from her shoulders, the wig ripped loose, her painted face shattering against the floor. From the pieces seeped a black tar that spread across the boards like oil, coating the wood and filling the room with the stench of rot.

Ford was crushed in silence. His small form bent backward until the wood snapped. From the split frame came a wetness that gleamed in the dim light, dripping from his arms as though his body were flesh after all. A drawing book fell open at his feet, its pages smeared in blood. Yet before the thick substance could take over, flashes of a drawn figure appeared before Melody's eyes. It resembled her, standing. Her torso was split in two and her guts spilled out. She was trying to hold them, but she didn't have the strength.

She tried to shake the image but couldn't.

Then came Baller. The Eggstabletman lifted him with both hands, his ragged arms trembling with the motion, and then brought him down upon the floor with a crack that shook the room. His limbs scattered. His head rolled across the boards to rest at Melody's bedside, the painted eyes fixed upon her.

She could not move.

The Eggstabletman stood among the wreckage. His hat shadowed his face, but she thought she saw the curve of his mouth, the suggestion of teeth bared in an unseen grin. Only thoughts.

His rags hung like funereal banners, black against the ruin of her family. The floor was slick with blood. The air was heavy with the smell of it. She lay frozen in her bed, heart hammering, her mouth open in silence.

He reached down for Baller's head. Lifted it, threw it on her chest. Blood splattered on her face. Up close, it looked more real than life itself.

Melody screamed herself awake. The nightmare melted into reality. The shape of the room shifted. From the darkness of before, to a lamp burning low on the dresser that for a moment she did not recognise because it wasn't her own. The shade cracked slowly, light thin as paper. Her skin was damp from the dream. Her chest still ached from the press of it. From Baller's head dripping with blood, eyes dead and still. She stared at the ceiling where the plaster was cracked into the shape of rivers.

Something shifted beside her.

"Bad dream?" Darcey asked.

"Yes," Melody nodded. "Did I wake you?"

Darcey turned her head. "No."

Melody pushed herself up on her elbows. "Another one," she said. "And I don't remember all of it. But it was bad. Worse than usual. I keep waking up like this. Every year."

Darcey looked away. Her mouth moved again, words too faint to catch. Then, louder, she said: "Dreams are just dreams."

"Not these," Melody shook her head.

Darcey smiled thin and shook her head. She pushed herself upright, wrapping her blanket around her shoulders. The bones of her hand showed sharp against the fabric.

"What do you see in them? You never told me."

"Shadows. Faces that aren't right. Things breaking. Blood. Lots of blood. Too much of it. God, I don't want to talk about it."

"Then don't."

They sat in silence. The old clock in the hall ticked. The radiator hissed once and went quiet.

"I talk to myself when it's bad," Darcey said. "Helps to hear something. Even if it's only me."

Melody nodded. "What do you say?"

"Nothing worth telling," Darcey shrugged.

The lamp hummed. A moth bumped against the shade and fell still on the floor.

"Do you ever think about the 20s Club?" Melody asked.

Darcey laughed dryly. "Everyone does."

"No," Melody shook her head. "Everyone talks about them. That's different. I mean *think*. Like actually think. What's the reason they're still together?"

Darcey shrugged. "They're just weirdos."

"Maybe they're not," Melody mumbled. "Maybe that creature they keep going on about is actually real."

Darcey's eyes flicked to the corner of the room. A shadow lay deep there. She bit her lip. "Or maybe they're just crazies."

"It could be," Melody dropped back down on her back, "but they're too scared. It feels too real."

"That's what they want you to think," Darcey hissed.

Melody watched her. Her friend mumbled again under her breath. Words too quick. Her eyes darted once more to that corner. Melody thought she heard her own name in those whispers but could not be sure.

"They still haven't found that girl, you know?" Melody said. "It's been years."

"Hard to find a kid lost in the woods."

"Doesn't seem to me like she just got lost."

"I don't know, Mel. That sort of talk creeps me out. Can we talk about something else?"

"Alright."

But they fell quiet. Outside, the wind rattled the trees. A car passed on the road with headlights cutting across the walls and gone.

"You ever given college a thought?"

Darcey shook her head. "Did you?"

"Not much up until the start of this year," she said. "I want to go away. Somewhere different. Somewhere I can dance."

Darcey looked at her. "With your leg?"

"I can get better," Melody said. "I have been getting better."

Darcey narrowed her eyes but said nothing.

"You don't think I can."

She shook her head. "The world doesn't care, Mel. Doesn't matter if you're good or not. Doesn't matter if you can or can't. You're gonna go to college to dance and it's gonna mean nothing. What does it matter if you're in a big city or if you're here?"

"It matters to me!"

"Why? What difference does it make?"

"Are you serious?"

"Yeah," Darcey nodded. "I am."

"Well..." Melody hesitated. "I...I don't know. Why does it have to make a difference? Why can't I just want something? Why can't you want something?"

"You know why," she spat.

Melody looked at her friend's hands clenched tight in the fabric. The faint tremor in her arms. "You're not broken," she said.

"Yes, yes I am."

The room seemed colder. The lamp hummed. The moth twitched once more and went still. Melody sank into the pillow. Her heart slowed but the unease did not leave her. She closed her eyes but still saw the mannequins breaking. The nightmare was coming back.

"Do you ever hear it when you're awake?" Darcey asked.

Melody's eyes opened. "Hear what?"

"Forget it," Darcey shook her head quickly.

"No. Tell me."

Darcey would not meet her eyes. "Just sounds. Like someone whispering. Sometimes...sometimes when I'm walking home. Sometimes when I'm lying here. Doesn't matter."

"What do they say?"

Melody's mouth felt dry.

Darcey pressed her lips together. "They tell me I'm theirs."

The words hung between them. Melody swallowed. She turned her face into the pillow. Darcey mumbled again, faster now. Her lips moved quickly, words spilling like a prayer. She rocked slightly where she sat.

"Idiot," she hit herself over the head. Not hard, but repeatedly. "Idiot. Idiot."

Melody reached out and touched her. "Darcey..."

She stopped. Darcey blinked at her, eyes wet. Her breath was uneven.

"It's nothing," Darcey said. "Just tired."

They lay in silence again. A long while. The clock ticked. The wind hissed against the window.

"I wish it would stop, too," Melody whispered.

Darcey stared at the ceiling. "It doesn't."

"You don't know that."

"Yes, I do."

Melody closed her eyes. "Then what do we do?"

Darcey pulled the blanket tighter, her face half hidden. "We wait."

"For what?"

"For it to come."

Darcey turned her head toward her. Her eyes were wide and dark.

"And you said the 20s Club were crazy."

"They are," Darcey nodded. "They are because they play-pretend. Why would you ever want to fake this sort of thing?"

"I don't know," Melody shook her head.

She stared deep into her friend's eyes and realized that those dark pools went deeper than she had ever seen them go before. She could see her own reflection in them. A struggle to remain on the surface.

The two of them lay together in the narrow bed, their noses almost touching, and the shadows pressed in around them like a weight too great.

The morning was pale and cold. Frost traced the windows of the bus. Melody sat near the back and watched the fields pass. Her body was heavy with sleeplessness. Darcey had been quiet when she left, her eyes shadowed, her lips moving still as though she prayed beneath her breath.

At school, the halls smelled of bleach and pencil dust. Students crowded the lockers, voices bouncing off the tiles. Melody walked slowly. She had given up her wheelchair at the start of the year, making use of two crutches. Her leg ached, but it didn't matter. Each step was one towards getting better.

Class did not matter to her that day. She had made up her mind about something the moment before falling asleep. She looked for them all throughout the school and only found them gathered together near a stairwell. A knot of boys and girls with their books slung loose, their voices sharp with conspiracy and laughter.

Melody stopped before them. She watched for a while, waiting to see if they would take note of her presence. But they were too deep into their own whispers. Too blinded by the rumours they themselves spread.

"You need to stop," Melody said.

The voices faltered. A girl with red hair tilted her head. "Go away," she hissed.

"I mean it."

"Yeah, you and all the others," Sam, the boy that shot her by accident those years back, said. "What difference does it make?"

"The difference is that I mean it," she said. "I'm not just telling you to make fun of you. All the stories and the games. All of it. You're not helping anyone. You're just feeding it."

The 20s Club looked at one another. A boy with freckles smirked. "What, are you scared?"

Melody's face hardened. "You don't get it at all," she shook her head. "Do you?"

"Just shove off, man," Sam turned to her. His hands were in his coat. He slowly stepped towards her.

"I'm tired of you guys," she continued, not caring for his approach. "Everyone is tired, and you can't see it. But they're not tired like me. And you know why? Because I get it. I know what you guys are talking about. So that's why I'm telling you to stop. You're only pretending. Making things up. Nothing of what you're saying is real."

"And who are you to say that?" Sam smirked. "People can't tell stories anymore?"

Melody narrowed her eyes. "Was Susie a story to you?" she asked. His smile vanished. "Was she 26, like you guys claim, when she vanished? She wasn't, right? So, what gives? How can you go on spewing stuff like that? Even after what happened. Can you not see yourselves? How stupid and heartless you all sound? You make everyone sick. Have you ever even thought about Susie's parents? About her friends when you keep on saying stuff like that?"

The group shifted uneasily. The red-haired girl crossed her arms.

"Girl, listen," she pouted. "We get you, alright? Shits messed up. But we didn't make it up. It was around long before us."

"Then let it die," Melody said. "If it was only a story then that's all it should be. A story. Nothing else."

Another boy leaned against the rail. "Why do you care so much? Nobody believes it anyway."

Melody's eyes darkened. For a brief moment, her nightmare played out before her. "That's a lie," she muttered. "There are those who believe it. That *know* it's true. The problem with you is that you *want* it to be true. You want to be the ones who know something no one else does. But you don't. It's just fear and make-believe. If what you actually said was true, you wouldn't be giddy about it."

They stared at her. Some frowned. Some looked away.

"You sound crazy," Sam muttered.

"You don't know what crazy is. You don't know what it feels like to wake up choking on it. You don't know what it does when it follows you from your dreams and into your days."

Her voice broke on the last word. She swallowed it down.

The red-haired girl shifted. "We're just messing around. It's not that serious."

"Yes, it is!" she shouted. "So, stop acting like it's not!"

The group was silent. The hall outside their circle hummed with other voices, students passing. Lockers slamming. But here it was still.

One boy at the edge spoke then. His voice quiet. Eyes downcast.

"I saw it."

They all turned to him.

He was small, his hair hanging into his eyes. He bit at his lip.

"I saw it," he said again. "In the dream. The hat. The rags. The nails. Just like we sing."

"Shut up, man," Sam spat.

But the small boy went on. "It was standing in the corner of my room, Sam," he shuddered. "I... I thought it was my dad, but it wasn't. It just stood there. Watching. When I looked at it too long, it shook its head. Just a little. Like... like it knew something."

Melody felt her chest tighten.

"You...you're lying," she mumbled.

"I wish I was."

The silence that followed was heavier than the noise that had come before it. The group looked from one to another, eyes darting, no one willing to speak.

The bell rang then, sharp and sudden. Students broke apart. The 20s Club gathered their books and slipped away in pairs and threes, bravado gone.

Melody stood alone by the rail. The sound of the bell echoed down the corridor, and in the dark pane of the window, she thought she saw for a moment the shape of a hat brim bent low, waiting.

Rain had passed in the night, leaving the world pale and damp. Morning light pooled on the ceiling in uneven patches, the color of watered milk. Melody lay in bed and watched the light change. Sometimes it made shapes—faces, rooms, doorways that opened and closed on their own. She had long ago stopped trying to decide whether they were tricks of the eye or something else.

Two years had passed since the performance. The memory of that night had faded into something that felt more like a dream.

She stared at the ceiling and thought *I used to be someone in motion.*

The room was quiet except for the low hum of a clock and the sigh of wind against the windowpane. The chair in the corner creaked once, though she hadn't moved.

She turned her head. He was sitting there.

The Eggstabletman, cross-legged, small and still, his hat casting a long shadow across the wall. He looked the same as always. She wasn't startled. The fear, in that moment, had worn off somehow. His presence felt inevitable, like the moon, or dreams she could never fully remember yet still feel.

"You've been quiet," he said. His voice smooth and low, unhurried. "Have you learned any poetry?"

She kept her eyes on the ceiling. "A little."

"It's been two years. Only a little?"

"Enough, I'd say. Rilke. Larkin." She thought for a moment, then added, "And Bishop. But it didn't do much. Reading doesn't make people see you. Especially not people like Vince."

"Did you even try to make him see you?"

Melody didn't say anything.

"That's fine," he sighed. "But reading poetry doesn't have to be about others. It can teach you to see yourself, too."

"That's overrated."

The chair creaked again. When she glanced over, she saw his clawed fingers drumming lightly on the armrest, almost human in their fidgeting.

"Do you remember what I told you that night?" he asked. "That poetry is rhythm? The pulse between silence and sound?"

"I remember."

"Did you keep that in mind? Learn anything from it?"

"Sure," she said. "I learned that I don't have rhythm. At least not one anyone hears."

He laughed. "You're too hard on yourself. You've always been. You danced and they watched. That's a rhythm."

"It had been once. I haven't danced in a while."

He tilted his head, the hat brim moving slightly. "You sound more troubled than usual."

She smiled faintly, not from amusement but exhaustion. "Is that your diagnosis?"

"You wear your unease like perfume. It fills the room. There," he said. "That better?"

Melody hesitated. "I suppose I am troubled. But not by what you think."

"Not the boy?"

She shook her head. "Vince is just a ghost now. It's something else. It's...Darcey."

His fingers stilled. "Your friend."

"Yes. She's been...different lately. She talks to herself more. Stares off. Sometimes she hums these strange tunes. Says she doesn't remember afterward."

He said nothing.

Melody turned to face him fully now. "I think she has one. Like you."

He didn't move.

"I've seen the way she flinches at shadows. The way she looks at the corners of rooms like something's hiding there. She won't tell me what's wrong, but I know. I feel it."

Still silent.

"You're not denying it," she said.

His voice came slowly, careful. "The world has many mirrors."

"That's not an answer."

"It's the only one worth giving."

She sat up, pulling the blanket around her shoulders. "So, it's true. There are others."

He didn't respond, but the faint tremor in the air between them was answer enough.

"Is she in danger?" Melody asked.

He tilted his head again, and for a moment she thought he might actually tell her something honest. But instead, he said: "Danger is a relative thing. Some are freed by it."

"You mean destroyed."

"Destroyed, freed—sometimes they are the same."

Her voice sharpened. "Don't play with words, Mr. Poet."

He regarded her, and in the small distance between them, the light shifted. For a heartbeat, she saw his face beneath the shadow—not fully, but enough to glimpse smooth, colorless skin and the faint curve of a mouth that didn't seem cruel at all.

"You care for this friend," he said.

"I do."

He nodded slowly, as though confirming a calculation. "Then help her."

"How?"

"By not letting her drown in fear."

Melody frowned. "What does that mean?"

He leaned forward slightly, elbows on knees. "When people begin to see the shape of their own darkness, they reach out for mirrors. But mirrors only show what's already there. Your friend may see something that looks like me, but it isn't. It's hers. You can't light it for her."

The words made her uneasy. "You talk like you're not real."

He smiled. She could feel it even if she couldn't see it.

"Reality is only the most agreed-upon dream," he said.

She sighed and lay back down, the blanket slipping from her shoulder. "You're avoiding the question."

"I'm keeping you safe."

"From what?"

He didn't answer. The wind pressed harder against the window. Rain had started again, a quiet percussion against the glass.

Melody closed her eyes. "You make things sound beautiful, even when they're not."

"It's a habit, perhaps."

For a time, neither spoke. The rain filled the pauses between their breathing. She thought about Darcey, her friend's hollow eyes, the way she had started drawing circles on her wrists with a pen whenever she got nervous.

"Do you think she'll be okay?" Melody asked at last.

"Do you want her to be?"

She frowned. "Of course."

"Then she will."

The words carried a strange finality, as though saying them made them true.

"You're lying," Melody said. He didn't deny it.

She opened her eyes again. The ceiling had darkened; the shapes she'd seen before had rearranged themselves into something that almost looked like wings spread wide.

"Sometimes I wish I'd never met you," she said quietly.

He stood, the movement slow, the shadow of his hat sliding across the wall. "And yet you keep calling me back."

"I don't call you."

"You do. Every time you start to fall apart, you whisper my name without meaning to. You build me out of your longing."

"That's not true, "she said, her throat tightening.

"Everything that matters is."

She wanted to argue but found no words. Her body felt heavy again, the weight of her sleeplessness returning.

He crossed to the window and looked out at the rain. "You've grown," he said softly. "Not in body, but in awareness. You see more now. That's dangerous."

"Then teach me how to live with it."

"Too much," he said, shaking his head. "And besides, I already am."

"You could help Darcey too. If she's really in danger, you could stop it."

"I could."

"But you won't."

He shook his head. "I am not her keeper."

"You're not mine either."

"Not yet," he said, almost tenderly.

Something cold moved through her chest. "Don't talk like that."

He stepped closer to the bed. The smell of rain followed him. "You misunderstand me, Melody. But I won't explain it to you now. You will see."

"What do you get out of it anyway?"

He tilted his head. "Everything."

She shivered.

He reached out then, not to touch her, but to brush a strand of hair away from her face, the movement impossibly gentle. His hand hovered there for a moment before lowering to his side.

"You're tired," he said.

"I don't want to sleep."

"Then don't."

She laughed softly, a sound closer to a sob. "You make it sound easy."

"Everything is easy," he said.

He stepped back toward the chair. The rags of his coat barely whispered as he moved.

"Tell me something, before you go," she said. "Will she die?"

"Darcey?"

"Yes."

He paused. "Everyone does, eventually."

"That's not what I mean."

"No," he said. "It isn't."

He sat again, folding himself neatly, hands resting on his knees. "Sleep if you can. Morning will be simpler."

"I doubt that."

He chuckled softly.

The rain outside thickened to a steady hiss. She turned her face into the pillow, the scent of detergent and damp fabric filling her nose.

When she looked again, the chair was empty. Only the faint indentation on the cushion remained, as if something had just risen from it.

The ceiling had gone blank. The shapes were gone.

Melody lay there for a long time, listening to the rain. She whispered a line from Rilke, half-forgotten. Then she closed her eyes and dreamed of mirrors.

5

THE END OF A WORLD

The stage belonged to Melody. She basked in a lone limelight, shining down from who-knows-where. There was no ceiling to the room. There were no walls but darkness. She did not fear. She had the dance. It was going to keep her going.

Not even when she saw him standing in the darkness did she falter. His red, glaring eyes. Two balls of flame growing larger. They'd swallow everything up.

Melody started, all on her own. She twirled and the darkness spun together with her. The two flames dragged on. A crowd appeared. But it was no ordinary crowd. The crowd was Ford and Baller and her parents too. Sets of them. One after the other. Clones upon clones. And these were not made of wood. Not like those before. These were flesh and bone. Their eyes glinting rhinestones in the dark.

The Eggstabletman danced between them. He twirled as she twirled but when her hands stretched out to grasp the air, the Eggstabletman's clawed at the crowd. Sharp nails cutting through flesh. Maiming features that she held so dear.

No! She tried to scream but the girl had no voice. *No! Stop!*

She did not speak to the creature, but to herself. Yet she could not. His red-flamed-eyes locked onto her and did not let her go. She spun and spun and with her he spun, too. Further and further, slicing through the crowd.

The scent of fresh-spilled iron clung to her nostrils. It choked and dragged tears out of her. She could not stop crying. Could not stop dancing. She twirled and hopped and watched him do the same, going through her family, one after the other.

They remained silent. As their faces got sliced through and their bodies dropped, lifeless, into the dark, they made no sound but that of their blood spurting out.

Her body ached. And yet she spun. She hopped and came to a temporary standstill, starting on again. Until she was hurt. Until the muscles snapped and the tendons ripped. Until her bones grew weak and shook. Until they could take no more and they started to break.

She winced and stumbled, but she could not stop. Her shins splintered. The bone tore through her flesh and bled all around her. She pranced, jaggedly, through puddles of her own blood. Her knees weakened. She stumbled and fell and dipped in the thick, drowning puddles. Blood. Blood. Blood. Family. Dead. Baller. Ford. Melody. Victor. India. Dead. Dead. Dead. All dead. Dying. Dead and dying. Dance. Dance. Dance.

"For me," the voice said. "Dance for me. Dance. Dance. Dance. You stop, they die. Not here, but everywhere. Dance! Dance! Dance!"

And she danced, breaking and crying, bleeding and dying, until nothing remained.

Melody was to attend her high school prom all by herself. No one had dared invite her. Ford had suggested that he could come as her partner, but Melody wanted to spare him from embarrassment.

The gym had been stripped and cleaned, banners draped across the rafters, the smell of wax and perfume and too many bodies. Lights spun slow from the disco ball, flashing across faces made strange by the shimmer. Someone had spilled fruit punch, and it bled red down the tiles. Melody stood at the edge of it all, hands at her sides, her dress a pale blue that caught the color of the lights and shifted like water when she moved.

She had told her parents she was going with a group. By the time she arrived, everyone had already become pairs. She stood with her back to the wall and watched them sway. Her heart beat too fast. The air was heavy with the sweetness of hairspray and sweat and the faint cheap ozone of the machine that made fog in corners.

It would've been good to laugh at herself if she could.

Someone brushed past her and said her name, but she didn't answer. The music was too loud. The bass thumped against her ribs. A slow song came on, and the couples drew closer. Boys in jackets too big for them. Girls in dresses that glittered when they turned. The world of eighteen pretending to be grown.

She thought of Darcey. Darcey had not come. She had stopped answering texts altogether, her silence thick as the fog spilling in from the corners of the hall. Melody had stood outside her house the week before and seen no lights on, curtains drawn, the mother's car gone. The house empty. She thought of that and of the dark in her own room and of the whisper that came when she closed her eyes.

The gym lights dimmed further, and the disco ball turned slower, scattering pieces of silver across the walls. Melody moved toward the edge of the floor. The music swelled and she saw her reflection in one of the panels of polished glass they had hung as decoration. For a moment, it was not her reflection at all.

Behind her stood that same figure. Torn rags. Hat low. Hands so long they touched the floor. The light caught the edge of a nail. She blinked. He was gone. But she knew better than to think he had left.

She turned her head slightly, and in the mirrored surface of the punch bowl, she saw him again, bent near the table, motionless.

She stepped away. Her hands trembled. The music changed again. Faster now. Laughter rising like smoke. She tried to steady her breath. And then he was beside her. No one saw. No one ever saw. He was close enough that the air chilled. His voice was the soft scrape of cloth across bone.

Go to him, the figure said.

She did not move.

Go on, the voice continued. *Go to him. You know who. You wanted to for so long. He's waiting for you.*

Her eyes moved across the crowd. Vince stood near the far wall, his tie loosened, his hair falling over his eyes. He was talking to a girl from the track team. His laugh broke through the music, easy and warm. The sound twisted something in her chest.

Go, the voice said. *She has nothing over you. You shared a smile. A touch. Remember. Remember. You can dance. He can sing. It's a match-made-in-abyss.*

Melody shook her head. He laughed at her.

Vince laughed too. The track-girl touched his arm and leaned in.

Hell forget you if you let him, whispered the Eggstabletman. *He's all that you have. All that you care about. Don't let it go.*

Melody's fingers clenched around the fabric of her dress.

You can change that. You can walk up. You can dance. I taught you. Do it. Do it. Don't be useless. Useless. Useless.

Her heart pounded harder. She looked toward the door, toward escape, but her legs did not move.

He'll never see you if you stay. Not unless you show him.

The music slowed. The crowd swayed in pairs. Melody stepped forward once, then again. She stumbled out of fear. Her legs were steady. He was right. She knew how. How to walk and how to dance. It was more than anything she'd had before. Her shoes scuffled the floor. The air smelled of sweat and roses. She crossed the gym floor one measured step at a time, her eyes on Vince.

He turned then, mid-laugh, and saw her.

For a moment, something passed across his face—surprise, confusion, a ghost of recognition. He smiled, faintly, uncertain, the way people do when they're not sure if they remember you from a dream.

Melody stopped a few feet away. Her mouth was dry. The music pressed down heavy and slow.

"Hi," she said, the word small.

He nodded once. "Melody, right?"

She nodded. "Hey. What's up?"

She hadn't known he still remembered her name. The sound of it in his voice loosened something inside her.

"You look nice," he said.

"Thanks."

The girl beside him looked from one to the other, then touched Vince's arm and said she'd get drinks. She left with a smile too wide.

They stood in the wash of colored light.

"It's been a while," Vince said.

"Yeah."

She could feel the Eggstabletman behind her, his breath cold along the back of her neck, the faint whisper of his existence ever-present.

"Didn't think you'd come," he said.

"I wasn't sure either."

He smiled. "Glad you did."

The song changed again, another slow one, the kind written to break hearts.

"Do you want to dance?" he asked.

Her mouth opened, but the words caught. "What—what about the girl?"

"Ah, she'll be fine," he waved the thought away. "So?"

She looked over her shoulder. A scarce few couples were there. A shimmer of the disco lights spilling across the floor.

She turned back to him. "I—"

You do! Dance. Dance. Dance.

Melody nodded.

"Sweet."

They stepped onto the floor. His hand light at her waist, hers on his shoulder. The world spinning in silver and shadow. She felt the weight of her leg, the stiffness there more than ever, but she moved anyway. The music swelled. Around them, others swayed and turned, laughter echoing from the corners.

For a brief moment, she forgot the voice, the shadows, the long nights of cold whispers. She felt almost human again.

Then she caught a glimpse in the disco balls' turning facets—a flash of dark cloth. He took Vince's place. He was there, holding her, spinning her, drawing her close.

Her step faltered. Vince looked at her. Drew her back. "You, okay?"

"Just dizzy."

"Want to stop?" he asked.

"No. No. Please..."

The ball turned again, and they turned with it. The reflection was gone. She breathed deep and tried to keep moving. When the song ended, he smiled and thanked her, polite, uncertain, and then walked away.

Melody did not want to let go of his hand. The lights flashed. The music changed. And she held him.

"What's up?" he asked.

"Do you mind if we talk a little?"

In the reflection of the gym doors, she saw the Eggstabletman watching her from the shadowed hall. He raised one hand as if tipping his hat. She smiled, faintly, though she did not know why.

"Talk? What about?"

Melody shook her head. "Just talk. The two of us. Just for a little. Is that okay?"

Vince looked over his shoulder, as if in search of someone.

"Sure," he sighed. "Come on, we'll go outside."

The air was cool and smelled of rain that never came. The parking lot lights buzzed high above them, halos of yellow cast across the asphalt. Crickets somewhere in the grass. Music still faint behind the doors.

Vince sat down on the curb. He looked up at her, playing with his tie. He looked older out here, the sharpness of the dance gone from him. Melody looked at his face and in it she saw the future. She wasn't sure whether she liked what she saw there, that far away. But here in the present, it was all good.

"So, what's up? You sure you're good?"

"Mhmm..." she nodded.

"You looked a little pale back there."

"Too hot," she said. "Too many people."

He nodded. "You want to walk?"

"Where would we go?" she asked.

"Nowhere. Anywhere. Just away, I guess."

Melody nodded. He stood up and they walked. The lights from the gym grew small behind them. Ahead, the lot sloped down toward the back field where the grass was cut short and silver in the half-light. Beyond it, the trees. A lazy sway in them, like brush strokes.

They found a bench near the old baseball diamond. The metal cold through the thin fabric of her dress. The moon was up but thin, washed behind the clouds. A wind came across the field and moved her hair.

Vince sat at the far end of the bench. His hand brushed against his knee, restless.

"I always forget how quiet it gets out here," he said.

"It's better than inside."

"Yeah?" He looked at her. "You're the type of girl to like the quiet, aren't you?"

She nodded.

"I remember you sitting outside the gym after practice while everyone else was losing their minds."

"I had no choice," she muttered. "You know, my leg."

"Right," he grimaced. "Sorry."

"It's okay."

They sat in silence. The wind passed through the trees. A car revved its engine somewhere in the distance.

"You're a good dancer, you know?" he said. "You got better since the talent show."

"You remember that?"

"Of course."

"I thought it was only me."

"You're a brave girl, Mel. In your place, well, I don't think I would've gone up on that stage."

"That's silly," she blushed. "You play music in front of people."

"It's different. I'm popular. The people want me up there. I could go and sit still and they'd watch me. It's sad, really. It's like it doesn't even matter that I can play. But you. Well. You won some of them over with your dance alone. You won me. Then and tonight, too."

Her eyes lit up.

"What are you doing after high school?" he asked. "College?"

Melody lowered her head. "There's nothing I'm good at."

"Dancing," he said. "You're good at dancing."

"There are no colleges for that."

"Of course there are. I'm going to one. It's the next state over. Not too far. It's pretty good, too. You should look into it."

"You think I'd get in?"

"God, they'd be stupid not to take you," he said. "I'm serious. What about your friend? That other girl. What was her name?"

"Darcey."

"That's it."

"You know about her?" She looked confused.

"I've been trying to. She didn't seem to be in a good place. I try to help people like that when I can." He hesitated. "I had an older brother," he said. "He had the same look on his face."

"What do you mean?"

"That pale stare that your friend has. That you had for a moment when we were dancing."

"Oh, Vince, it was nothing. I promise you."

He shrugged. "Maybe. But that's what he said, too, and he's not here anymore. He was only 26, you know, when he went. That's funny, isn't it?"

"What? No, it's not."

"I don't mean him dying," he waved the idea quickly away. "I meant that group of kids. You know them? The 20s Club? Maybe they're onto something."

"Don't say that," she muttered. "They're just making stuff up."

"Sure, Mel. I didn't mean to pry or anything."

Melody shook her head. "Did your brother ever mention any strange dreams?" She asked. Tone low. "Like something that won't leave him alone?"

"Nightmares, you mean?"

"Something like that."

He looked at her profile in the dim light. "Yeah. At the beginning, when he was younger. But as he went on, he mentioned them less and less."

Melody frowned, not knowing what to say.

Vince hunched down and picked up a rock from under the bench. He threw it toward the outfield fence. It clicked against the metal and dropped into the dark.

"You know," he said, "when I was a kid and I watched my brother, I used to think that something lived all around him. Like a ghost or whatever. I'd see things move over his shoulder."

"What else?"

"Nothing else," he shrugged, looking for another rock. "I'm sure it was just in my head."

"And if it wasn't?"

"Don't start with that," he grinned.

But she didn't smile. Her eyes were fixed on the dark line of trees beyond the fence. The hum of the light seemed louder now. She could feel the air shift around her, like the world had taken a breath. In the reflection of the dugout window, she thought she saw something move. A shadow over the world's shoulder.

She blinked, and it was gone.

Melody turned to look at him. He had found a rock but held it in his hand, rolling it. *Get closer,* the voice said. He was there. *Go in. Hold him. Look, he needs it.* But she couldn't do it. She had thrown him into a dark place.

She rose to her feet.

"We done?" he asked.

Melody nodded.

"Want me to walk you home?"

"No, it's okay."

He rose, too. They walked a little way toward the field. The grass wet around their shoes. The smell of it sharp. The clouds were breaking now, and the stars were just beginning to show through.

"It's weird. After tonight, it's like everything's ending. We'll all go some-where different."

"That's how it's supposed to go."

"The end of the world," he said. "Feels strange."

She nodded. "It does."

They stopped near the edge of the outfield fence. The school behind them just a dim block of brick and windows. The music from the gym carried faintly across the air. Warped and distant.

Vince looked at her again. "Hey," he said.

"What?"

"See you in college?"

She hesitated. "My parents won't let me."

"You're an adult now, Mel. You can do whatever you want."

"Maybe," she smiled. She didn't think about it like that. "I don't know. I'll see."

"I'll be sad if you're not there. I'll look all over campus for you."

She blushed. "Okay. Fine. I'll apply. Give me the name."

And he did. "Good luck," he said.

"You too."

And he was gone.

He started back toward the lot. She stood and watched until he was gone. The wind came again, carrying the smell of asphalt and rain. The lights flickered once and steadied.

Melody turned toward the dark trees and saw him there—the faint outline of a small figure under the bleachers, hat low, rags shifting in the wind.

From somewhere inside her came that same quiet, bitter whisper that sounded so much like her own voice.

I told you.

The wind died. The field fell still.

She stood there a long time in the dark, the music long faded, the stars bright and cold above her.

6

NEW BEGINNINGS; SAME OLD WORLD

She wakes up in a confessional box. Through the lattice wall, she can see the other compartment. At first, it was dark and empty. And then those red eyes. Peering through, right at her.

"It's bad out there," he said.

"What is?" she asked.

"Death. It's everywhere. It's come for those you love."

"What? No."

"Look, if you don't believe me."

The far wall of his compartment opened up as if a window. Past it, darkness. A figure draws near. India, her mother.

"Leave her alone."

"She gets run over," he said.

Through the darkness, a car. The roar of its engine and the squeal of its brakes and then *splat*. The burst of blood and organs. Her mother gone. Nothing was left of her but memory.

"God!" Melody gasped. She tried to look away but strings attached to her head. They held her still. Did not let her turn elsewhere. "Stop this!"

"Little Fordie next," he said. "You ready?"

"Please! You don't have to do this! Let them be! It's me you want, right? It's me! Just take me!"

"Not yet. You're not ready. Look at Fordie. Look who is next to him."

It was her father. He stood there, arms crossed, head low and dejected.

"Is that all you can do?" the father asked. His voice was distant and warped, as if he spoke through water. But Melody, she could understand. "Just draw? You're a man," he raised his voice. "Men don't draw. I need help on the farm. With your mother gone..."

Ford continued to draw.

"Listen to me!" Victor lunged and hit the boy across the face. He fell backwards. Fear deep-set in his eyes. "Damn you! Look what you made me do! Why won't you listen?"

"I just want to draw!" Ford whimpered. "I want to draw Melody! That's all I want to do!"

"That damn girl again! Don't mention her name around here! She left us! She went to college in that sorry state she was in! Don't you even bring her up!"

"But she's my sister. I love her!"

Rage took hold of Victor. He fell upon his son, large hands around his neck. He squeezed hard, the boy writhing in despair.

"No! Dad! Stop! I'll come back! I'll come back! Leave Ford alone! God—no—oh—God!"

She banged her fists against the latticed divider. No use. The neck snapped and Ford's movements stilled in an instant. Victor drew back.

"Oh God..." he gasped. He looked at his hands. Then at Ford. Then back at his hands. "What...what did I do...what..."

He turned and walked into the darkness. Melody looked on. Waited. The father returned. He held a double-barrel in his hand. He sat down, cocked it, placed the barrels in his mouth and shot.

Melody roared. She watched him slump. She listened to the drip of blood. It was never ending.

"Don't look away now. There's Baller, still."

She looked through tear-filled eyes. She waited. And waited. And waited for the horror to come. But it never did. Not until she heard a trap-door give way. Then rope unfurling. From the ceiling a body fell. Tied around its neck, a noose. He died instantly. Swung like a metronome, lifeless. Her eyes followed. Left. Right. Left. Right. Again, and again. The Eggstabletman laughed.

He laughed until she woke up.

The campus spread out before her like a half-remembered dream. Wide lawns, red brick buildings, trees shedding the last of their leaves into the wind. Melody walked slowly along the path, the strap of her bag across her shoulder. Her acceptance papers folded tight in the side pocket though she no longer needed them.

The scholarship had come late in the summer, a letter she'd half believed was meant for someone else. Her mother had cried when she read it. Her father had lifted her up from the kitchen chair and laughed until he couldn't breathe. She'd felt proud but not whole. And when she saw the name of the college, her heart had jumped. Vince's school. The thought of it had burned inside her like a secret.

Now she was here.

The morning light was thin, the color of milk. Students passed in groups, their voices soft, their laughter carried away by the breeze. She caught reflections of herself in the tall windows as she walked. The slight limp was still there. Even after all these years and with *his* help, she could not get rid of it.

She wore a puzzled look on her face. An uncertain expression she'd worn since she'd arrived. She tried to picture Vince somewhere among these buildings. She wondered if he would remember her. She wondered if he'd changed.

The clock tower struck the hour, and she turned down another path, her shoes tapping against the wet stones. A boy on a bike sped past, nearly clipping her, and called out an apology she barely heard.

At the center of the quad, she stopped. A fountain trickled, the sound soft and steady. She stood there a while, just watching the waterfall.

"Melody?"

She turned.

He was standing there, backpack slung over one shoulder, hair longer than she remembered, a small smile on his face like he wasn't sure if it belonged there.

"Vince," she said.

"Jesus, it is you," he said and laughed. "I told you you'd get in, didn't I? God, I—well, from the way we left off last time, I didn't think you'd come."

"You think I'd pass up a free ride?"

He shook his head. "You look different."

"So do you."

He came closer. He smelled faintly of soap and rain. "How long have you been here?"

"Just today. They're still giving me the runaround with housing."

"You'll get used to it," he said. "This place never knows what it's doing."

She laughed, quiet and real. It felt strange in her throat.

They stood there a moment longer, the sound of the fountain between them. He shoved his hands in his pockets. "You look good," he said. "Really good."

She flushed. "Thanks. I've been working on things."

"I can tell."

Her heart turned into a fluttering thing. It felt foolish to let it move her like that, but she couldn't help it. The light caught in his eyes, and she felt again the strange electricity of being eighteen on a gym floor, the reflection of the disco ball spinning above them.

"You got time later?" he said.

"Yeah," she answered quickly. "I do."

"I finish class around four," he said. "And after that I'm going out with some friends. I'd love for you to meet them. What'd'ya say?"

"I'd like that."

"Good," he smiled again. "I'll meet you at the student center?"

"Okay."

He hesitated a moment, then added. "It's really good to see you, Mel."

She nodded, unable to say more.

He waved once and walked off across the quad, his stride easy, his head turning once before he disappeared behind the line of oaks. She stood until he was gone. The wind lifted the edge of her coat. The fountain kept running, its water silver under the gray light. She watched her reflection waver on the surface. It rippled, twisted, then steadied again.

Her mind turned to Darcey. She had not seen her in almost a year. She had called and visited her house but nothing. She drew a slow breath. For the first time, the world felt far and small.

The clouds moved. The sun came through in brief pale beams. Students hurried past, laughing, calling to one another. The air smelled clean.

Melody sat on the stone lip of the fountain. She traced a finger through the water. Her hand shook a little, but she smiled anyway.

She told herself that things could begin again here. That whatever had followed her, whatever had whispered and watched, would stay behind. Even if the nightmares didn't.

She closed her eyes and let the sound of the water fill her head. The rhythm of it was almost music.

Somewhere, faintly, a bell rang.

The café was small and crowded, all brick and amber light, the air thick with the smell of coffee and rain from the street. Music played low from a speaker in the corner, an old song no one was really listening to. Melody sat at a table by the window, her coat folded across her lap, watching the drizzle trace thin lines down the glass. She was early. She'd always been early for things that mattered.

Vince arrived a few minutes later with three others in tow. He spotted her and smiled that same easy smile.

"Hey," he said. "You've seen my text, then?"

She nodded.

"You didn't say anything. I thought you didn't," he sat. "It was too rainy to meet at the initial spot and then walk here. It's better this way."

The others came forward. Two guys and a girl. They looked her over with the casual curiosity of people used to measuring new arrivals. The girl introduced herself first, a tall blonde with sharp eyes and a voice that tilted up at the ends of her sentences. "I'm Casey," she said. "We've heard about you."

Melody blinked. "You have?"

"I might've mentioned you," Vince said.

Casey smiled, her hand sliding onto Vince's shoulder. It lingered there a little longer than Melody would've liked. She sat down next to him.

The guys—Marcus and Theo—took their seats across from them. They were loud, full of jokes that tripped over one another, both wearing the same thin smiles.

Vince waved a server over and ordered a round of coffee.

Melody folded her hands together under the table. She could feel the faint tremor in her fingers.

The conversation started easy enough. Classes, professors, the terrible cafeteria food, stories about the dorms. Vince told one about a roommate who practiced guitar at three in the morning until someone pulled the fire alarm just to make him stop. Melody laughed with the others, although she did not find it all that funny.

As they talked, she noticed small things. The way Marcus kept glancing towards the dark corner of the café near the bathroom door. The way Theo picked at his sleeve like he was hiding something beneath it. Casey's laughter, too, dying at times all of a sudden.

Then Vince excused himself to grab some napkins and the table grew quiet.

Theo leaned back in his chair. "So, you're the hometown girl, huh?"

"Yeah," she said.

"Small world," Marcus smirked. "You both ended up here."

"Well," she frowned, throwing a brief glance at Casey, "it was actually his idea for me to come."

Casey perked up. "Was it?"

Melody nodded shyly. "I didn't think I stood a chance, but he talked me into it and well, here I am."

"Cool," Theo said as if he didn't listen. "Do you know about his brother?"

"Vince's?"

"Theo!" Casey hissed.

"What? It's nothing. If they're from the same town, then she knows. Right?"

Melody looked after Vince but could not find him. She didn't understand how it could take so long to find some napkins.

"He's told me, yes," she nodded.

"Which version?" Marcus smiled. "The one where he killed himself, or the one where he disappeared?"

Melody narrowed her eyes. "What do you mean, disappeared?"

"So, the former," Marcus nodded. "Well, I guess you're not as close as I thought."

Vince came back with napkins, grinning for a moment until he saw the look on Melody's face. "What did you guys do?" he asked. "Are you okay?"

"Just talking," Theo shrugged.

"Don't mind them, Mel," he nudged her shoulder. "They're a bit superstitious. So, if it's ghosts, they mentioned, or anything of the sort, you're better off covering your ears."

Vince laughed them off into a different subject.

Still, Melody couldn't shake the feeling that something was wrong. Dark and familiar. She tried not to pay it too much mind but when she looked up at the group, all she could see was Casey and the way her body tilted toward Vince. The way her hand brushed against his arm when she spoke.

"Not to bring it back or anything but we should do that thing by the lake Marcus mentioned," Theo glanced at Vince, then at Melody and smiled. "Bring the speaker some beers. Have a little get-together. What do you say?"

Vince turned towards Melody. "You don't have to say yes if you don't want to come."

"I'll come," she said. "It'll be nice, I'm sure."

The rain outside thickened into a soft downpour, the sound filled the café and made the lights seem dimmer. She caught her reflection in the window. Pale, distant, her eyes dull from the glare. And just behind her reflection, she thought she saw another shape.

She blinked and it was gone.

Casey's laughter broke her trance. Melody turned in time to see her leaning in close to Vince, whispering something against his ear. He smiled, said something back. Casey's face lit up. A moment later, their fingers laced together.

The conversation at the table moved on without her. She stared at the condensation crawling down her cup, at the ripple of her reflection warped by it.

By the time she looked up again, Casey was kissing him. Quick, soft, clumsy presses. When it ended, Vince's eyes found hers.

He smiled at her, eyes devoid of guilt. He gave her the faintest of shrugs. Then he looked away.

Casey laughed again, covering her mouth, pretending it was nothing. Marcus and Theo were already on their phones. The noise of the café swallowed them all.

When they stood to leave, no one said much.

"Good catching up with you," he said. "See you over the weekend at the lake?"

"Sure," she muttered.

Vince left with the others. The door closed behind them and the bell above it rang once, sharp and small. The world seemed to fall away from her. She sat alone at the table. The rain came down, steady and silver. Her coffee had gone cold.

For a long while she didn't move. She only watched the dark window and the lamplights bleeding through.

Then a whisper came.

"You, see?"

Her hand tightened around the cup.

"He was never yours."

She looked down. The reflection in the coffee shifted. His brimmed hat was there.

"Only I am," he said. "You have me. You have your dancing. That's all you need."

The sound of the rain grew louder. She closed her eyes.

"Dance for me again," he said. "Only for me. Dance and dance again."

The whisper faded. The café lights flickered once and steadied. She opened her eyes. The reflection was gone. But the feeling stayed, cold and familiar, pressing against her heart.

7

DANCE ON

She found herself in darkness. The air is thick and close. A weight on her chest. No sound but her own heart, slow and heavy as a drum in the deep. She lifted her hands and felt the wood above her, rough beneath her palms. The grain bit her skin. When she tried to move, there was nowhere to go. The sides of the box pressed against her arms and legs.

She drew breath and it came shallow. The air is dry, stale. Not enough. The smell of dirt and rot.

She struck the lid once with her fist. The sound was dull, swallowed by the weight of earth. She struck again until her hand split and the blood ran warm across her waist. No sound answered her. Only the stillness of the grave.

The dark had its own shape. It breathed. She felt it watching her.

Then came the sound of soil shifting. The scrape of nails through dirt. Above her, the wood creaked. A small crack of light appeared, thin as a blade, white and cold.

Something moved.

Two points of red burned through the opening. Eyes without shape. Eyes that saw without seeing. The light widened. She saw his hands first—long and gray, the fingers ending in curved nails black with earth and crusted blood. They pressed against the coffin lid and pulled it open as though it weighed nothing at all.

He bent over her. The hat is still on his head. The torn rags hanging from his shoulders. His face half-hidden in shadow, his breath the scent of dust and death. She could not see his mouth, but she felt the heat of it. It's hunger.

He leaned close until his brim brushed her forehead. His voice was a whisper of cloth through sand.

"What has no tongue yet speaks in the dark?"

She could not answer. Her throat was stone.

"What feeds when the heart sleeps and the sun turns its back?"

His hand found her arm. His fingers cold, the nails biting deep. He lifted it to the light, the pale flesh trembling. She tried to pull away but her strength was gone.

The rags shifted. Something moved beneath them. A sound like teeth grinding against bone. Then pain. He sank his mouth into her flesh. The skin tore. The blood ran hot. She felt the pull of it, the suction, the sound of him feeding slow and steady like an animal at a trough. She screamed but the sound never left her mouth.

He tore loose. Flesh came with it. He chewed once, twice. The sound was wet, obscene.

She then saw the cloth over his mouth. The splatter of blood. The bits of flesh, as if taunting her.

He spoke again, the words thick and slow.

"What is born without breath and dies without death?"

He laughed, low and broken. The sound of wood splitting. She turned her head. She could not move the rest of her body. The pain burned through her arm and into her chest. The blood filled the coffin, pooling beneath her.

He leaned closer, his hat shadowing her face. She felt his voice now. More than heard.

"You will dance when I tell you. You will bleed when I call for it. You are the rhythm. You are the hollow drum that will feed me."

He dragged his tongue along the wound, the touch of it cold as ice, sealing the gash though she still felt the pulse of pain beneath it.

The red eyes widened, glowing brighter. The coffin began to close again.

The earth fell soft and heavy. The sound of it is like rain. The last thing she saw was his face. A dark blur that seemed to grow ever-larger, as if to take over her own existence.

His voice came one last time.

"Riddle me the end, little dancer. What name shall the dark sing when all the lights are gone?"

The lid shut. The world vanished.

She felt the earth pressing down. She opened her mouth to scream but the dirt poured in. It filled   her throat, her lungs, her eyes. She tried to claw upward but her hands were gone, her arms leaden. The blood pooled around her face, warm and thick.

Somewhere above her, laughter. Not loud. Not wild. Just the sound of something satisfying.

Then silence.

She woke up gasping   .

The ceiling above her white and still. The sheets tangled around her legs. The air in the room is cold and thin. She sat up and felt the pain before she saw it.

Her right arm.

A bruise the size of a coin bloomed along the flesh near her wrist, dark and round, the edges marked by four faint crescents like the imprint of nails.

She touched it and felt the ache deep inside, not the kind of pain that comes from the body alone.

Outside her window the night was calm. The trees are unmoving. The campus is as dead as a nightmare.

She looked to the corner of the room and saw nothing there, though the shadows seemed to lean toward her. She pulled the blanket around her shoulders and sat that way until morning, the bruise throbbing faintly in time with her heartbeat.

When the first light came through the glass, it fell across her arm. The mark shone purple in the sun, and she thought she saw for an instant the faintest outline of teeth beneath the skin.

She turned her face away. But the whisper lingered still, soft and close, curling through her head like smoke.

You are the rhythm. You are the hollow drum.

She skipped all her classes that day. It wasn't like she was attending that many anymore anyway. Ever since she'd seen Casey and Vince kiss, the world had grown small. Nothing else mattered but the dancing.

In the end she didn't go with them to the lake. A few days after, Vince ran into her and probed her about it.

"Everything alright?" he asked.

"Sure," she said. She couldn't look him in the eyes.

He hesitated. "There's that thing again," he said. "That paleness."

"You're imagining things."

"Are you overworking yourself?" he asked. "Assignments piling up on you?"

Melody shook her head.

"Read anything lately?"

"What?"

He shrugged. "You're taking a literature seminar, right? Casey told me."

"Oh...sure. I'm reading."

"Do you like it?"

She looked up at him. "What are you trying to do here, Vince?"

"Woah," he drew back, "easy, Mel. I'm just trying to make conversation."

"I'm not in the mood for that."

"Was it something we did or said?" he asked. "You know, the guys like you. It might not seem like it, but they do."

"It's not them, either."

"Then me?" He paused. "It's me, right? The whole thing with Casey? Dammit. Listen, I should've said something. I mean...I didn't know it was like that for you, Mel. I really didn't. And you know how it is with girls, right? It's nothing and then it's something."

"Right..."

And that was that. The winter rolled on and came on hard that year. The wind across the campus carried dust and dry leaves, and the trees along the main walk stood bare and black against the gray sky. The students hurried between buildings with their coats pulled tight, their laughter carried off in little clouds of breath. Melody watched them from her window. The glass was cold beneath her palm.

A day of skipped classes turned into two. Two into three. And three into all. The professors sent her emails, her phone filled with reminders. She left them unopened. She told herself she would start again tomorrow, then the next day, and then she stopped saying even that. The books stayed stacked on the desk, untouched, the pages curling at the edges from the dry heat of the radiator.

The only time she moved was when she danced.

She would push the bed aside and clear the narrow floor of her dorm room, pull the curtains closed, and let the stillness settle. She no longer needed music. Or the eyes of all her dancing colleagues. The rhythm and attention came from somewhere else, from the pulse that lived behind her ribs. From *him.*

She moved slowly at first, her body heavy, her legs unsteady with heartbreak, and then faster, until the pain became its own language.

She told herself it was practice. That she was getting stronger.

Outside, life went on. She could hear it through the thin walls. The laughter in the hall, the doors slamming, the sound of someone playing a guitar two rooms down. It all seemed far away, as if she were listening to another world through a wall of glass.

Sometimes she stood at the mirror and looked at herself. The circles under her eyes, the pallor of her skin. She looked exactly like what Vince feared. She traced the bruise on her arm with her fingertips. It remained there, not subsiding no matter how many weeks passed.

At night she dreamed of the coffin, of the red eyes peering down. She woke up gasping, the sheets damp, her heart beating hard enough to shake her chest. She would rise and stand before the window and watch the lights across the quad, the silhouettes moving between them. She told herself that she was awake, that she was safe, though she no longer believed in either.

At the beginning she thought of Vince. She thought of how he had told her to join the college just to go and spoil everything.

She missed her family but could not bring herself to call. The idea of their voices felt unbearable. The warmth of them, the worry. She imagined her mother in the kitchen, the smell of onions and bread, her father coming in from the fields. Ford drawing at the table.

The world narrowed to the room. The pale walls, the single window, the clock that had long since stopped ticking. The smell of dust and old paper. She began to lose sense of the days. Sometimes she woke to find the light already gone.

When she did leave, it was only to walk the campus paths at dusk. The air is sharp and cold. The lamps flickering one by one. The sound of her shoes on the stones was the only sign that she existed.

The faces she passed were strangers now. Some nodded. Most didn't.

She felt herself thinning, like a photograph worn down by too many hands.

In her room she danced and danced and danced again. Slow starts, with faint catches of breath. Then she would feel it, that other presence—his—like hands guiding her shoulders, a rhythm not her own. She moved with it until her legs gave out. She fell once, twice, again, until her knees bruised and her palms burned. Then she would lie there, staring at the ceiling, her breath ragged, her heart echoing in silence.

The whispers came softer now, but they came all the same. Sometimes she could almost make out words. Sometimes they were only sounds, half-formed, like a song hummed from another room.

She began to hum with them.

When she slept, she dreamed of movement—endless turning, her body weightless and hollow. The sound of a hat brushing against her hair.

She woke each morning with her muscles aching, her feet sore, though she could not remember leaving the bed. The bruise on her arm darkened some more, the shape shifting, like a moving mouth.

One morning she caught her reflection in the mirror and hardly knew herself. The eyes too pale, the face drawn thin. She smiled without meaning to.

The light outside the window was gray. Snow had begun to fall, thin and slow. It gathered on the sill, melted, and gathered again. She watched it for a long time, unmoving.

Somewhere beneath her, in the hall, laughter rang out. It faded quickly.

She turned away from the window and pressed play on the small speaker on her desk. The music came faint and distant, but the rhythm was enough. She moved her bed back, cleared the floor once more.

Her feet found the pattern before her mind did. The steps coming from memory, or from somewhere deeper than that.

Outside, the snow kept falling, soft and soundless. The lights along the path flickered, then steadied.

She danced on, waiting for the song to end. But it kept on coming, without stopping.

8

CASEY

he sky was the color of rusted iron, a lid clamped over the world. The land stretched flat to every side, a red plain without horizon, its soil damp beneath her feet as if the ground itself was bleeding. No wind, no sound. Only the pulse of her own heart, loud and slow, the rhythm of something hunted.

She knew he was there before she saw him. The air changed and grew colder. A figure stood far off, gray and small, the hat low over the face, the shape of it wavering like heat. She tried to move, but it was as though the plain slowed her down. Each step sank, her feet swallowed by the earth as though it wished to keep her.

When The Eggstabletman began to walk, the sky darkened. The distance between them folded in on itself until he was close enough that she could hear the dry whisper of his rags brushing the soil. He did not hurry. He had no need.

She raised her hands. There was nothing to hold. The air around her thickened, humming with some low note she felt more than heard. The light dimmed to the color of dried blood. When he reached her, he did not speak. His hat brim touched her cheek. The smell of him was dust and grave earth. His hand closed around her wrist, and in that touch was the cold of long-lost centuries.

Pain flared—quick, electric—though she saw nothing. No teeth, no nails. Only the sense of flesh yielding, of something drawn from her. She twisted, striking at him, but her arms were weak, her blows landing soundless against the rags. The humming grew louder, filled her skull, pressed her thoughts to nothing.

She stumbled back. The plain tilted under her feet, the ground rippling like muscle. He followed, slow, certain. His head tilted as if listening to something deep below them. When he reached for her again, she snatched a branch from the soil—she did not know how it was there, a dead limb jutting from the earth—and swung.

The wood struck his shoulder with a dull crack. The hum ceased. He folded backward into the haze, swallowed by the red light. The air went still. She stood gasping, her arm slick with something warm, though the wound itself was invisible.

The plain began to fade. The sky lightened to gray. She fell to her knees, pressing her hand to the mark he'd left. The pulse beneath it beat in time with her own.

Then the ground gave way, and she was falling. Falling through the red light and into blackness.

Days passed like shadows lengthening across a wall. Melody stayed in her room. The blinds drawn, the air stale with the smell of coffee gone cold. She moved a little. The bruise on her arm had turned a deep purple, then yellow, then faded to something that wasn't gone but buried beneath the skin.

Classes went on without her. The world outside the window changed light but not shape. Students passed through it like figures in another life.

Their voices rose and fell; laughter, footsteps, the steady hum of a world she no longer belonged to.

Her phone rang often. Always her mother.

"Mel," she'd say, her voice carrying too much hope. "We haven't heard from you. How's school?"

Melody would hold the phone against her ear and wait for the right words.

"It's going fine," she'd say.

"You sound tired. Are you sleeping?"

"Yeah."

"You sure? Your father says you ought to—"

"I'm fine, Mom. I really am."

Silence. The kind that carries worry inside it. Then a sigh. "Okay, sweetie. We love you. Call home sometime, okay?"

"Sure…"

She hung up before the voice could say anything more.

Her father called once, his voice rougher, steady as old wood. He didn't ask questions. Only said he missed her, that Ford had started drawing monsters again, that Baller might come home for one of the summers, yet was not yet sure which. He told her to eat well, keep her head down, that they were proud of her.

She listened to it all without making a sound.

When the line went quiet, she held the phone to her chest for a long while, listening to the faint hum inside it, as if the voice was still there, just too far away to reach.

The nights grew longer. She kept the lights low, afraid of the shadows but more afraid of what might not be in them. She danced sometimes, half-asleep, the movements small, her body remembering the rhythm on its own. The air seemed to hum when she did. The pulse of the dream still lingered somewhere in her bones.

The calls slowed.

One evening, as dusk gathered outside, her phone lit up again. The name on the screen froze her. Vince.

Her breath caught. For a moment she could hear his voice before she even answered. The way he laughed, the soft carelessness in it. She stared at the glow of the name until it blurred.

The phone kept ringing. She thought of the dream. Of the eyes in the dark. Of the voice that had promised to find her again. The air around her felt thick. The pulse in her arm began to ache.

She let the phone ring until it stopped. The silence afterward felt like something closing its hand around her throat. She sat on the edge of the bed, the screen still glowing faintly in the dark. The name faded. The room fell still.

Outside, wind pressed against the window, soft and patient.

She whispered to no one but herself. *I'm fine.* Again, and again until she no longer had a voice.

The ringing did not stop. At first it came in intervals, hours apart. She would watch the name light the screen, wait for it to fade. Then it came faster. The silence between the calls shrinking until they felt like breaths. Each time it was him.

The sound of it grew unbearable. She turned the phone face down on the desk. Still, it lit the wall with its weak glow. Still, it hummed against the wood.

Once she answered. Said nothing. Listened. His voice was there, faint through the static.

"Mel. Please pick up. Just talk to me."

She pressed the phone close, her throat tight, but no words came.

"Are you okay?" he asked. "Just say something. Anything."

She ended the call and sat listening to the quiet whine of her own pulse.

After that she let the battery die. I watched the light fade. A relief, though a small death.

The days blurred on. She slept little. The air in the dorm grew stale, thick with the smell of her own stillness.

Then came the knocking. Soft at first. Two slow raps against the door. She froze, listening. The sound came again, louder, then stopped.

"Melody?"

His voice was coated in panic.

"Melody, I need to know that you're in there," he said and knocked again. "Just give me a sign."

Silence.

He knocked again. Faster this time. "Open up. Please. Please, please, please be in there."

She sat on the bed, staring at the door, her hands clutching at the blanket.

"Please," he muttered. "I've been trying to reach you. Your phone—God—" His voice broke, "It's important, Mel."

Still, she did not answer.

He hit the door. "Something's happened and I need to know that you are still in there. Please? Not you, too. Okay? I—I can't deal with this on my own and Theo and Marcus are not the best to have around right now. They're great, but—" He stopped. "Casey's gone. Nobody's seen her in a week."

The words fell like stones in the quiet room.

Gone.

He kept talking, the words blurred by the door, by her own heartbeat. "She left her things. Her roommate says she never came back from a party. They're looking everywhere. I've been looking, too. It's just—it's just like that time. With my brother. I—God, just open up. Please, just open up. Or at least, tell me you're still here."

She closed her eyes. The room tilted. She saw the dark brim of a hat, a figure in the fog of her mind. Whispers came for her: *Next time!*

"I don't know what to do, Mel..."

His voice was small now, almost afraid.

She rose halfway, one hand on the bedpost. The air around her felt heavy, as though the walls leaned closer to listen. He knocked one final time.

Nothing moved. Only the faint hum of the radiator, the low moan of the wind outside. At last she heard his footsteps fading down the hall. The echo lingered long after he was gone.

She sat back on the bed, her pulse still trembling in her wrist. The room seemed darker. Somewhere in that dark, a whisper materialised. Soft, pleased, patient.

Another dancer enters the stage.

The search for Casey went on for weeks. From her window, Melody watched them—clusters of students, campus police, volunteers—moving across the fields and wooded paths with flashlights cutting through the gray. Their voices reached her room in scattered fragments, the sound of people pretending hope was something that could be found if you only looked long enough.

Casey's face was everywhere now. The posters stapled to light poles, taped to doors, hung crooked from noticeboards. A photograph of her smiling in good light, hair caught by a summer breeze, a name and the word *missing* in thick black paint.

Melody looked at those eyes and saw nothing. Not cruelty, not kindness. Just absence. A life suspended between before and after.

At night she could hear the searchers returning. Boots scraping, voices low. The sound of exhaustion. The sound of failure. The air outside was heavy with rain that never quite came.

When she left the dorm, it was always late. The campus is quiet, the buildings pale and hollow under the lamps. She walked the paths alone, her breath clouding in the air. Sometimes she stopped at one of the posters and touched the paper, the cold dampness of it, as if to prove it was real.

The bruises on her arm darkened and grew. Wrapped around from wrist to shoulder, faint shapes within—fingers, the ghost of a grip.

The woods lay behind the athletic fields. A black line against the sky. She heard people say Casey had gone there.

Melody found herself walking there. The air grew colder as she neared the trees. The path thinned, the lamplight fading behind her. The smell of damp leaves and old bark filled her lungs. She stopped at the edge, the forest before her nothing but a wall of dark.

She could hear the hum of insects, the creak of branches rubbing together. Beneath that, another sound. Soft, almost human.

A pull.

It was not wind or instinct. It was a feeling low in her chest, a thread drawn tight between her and something unseen. The same tug she had felt in her dreams, the same voice that had guided her through shadow.

She stepped forward.

The ground wet and cold beneath her shoes. The darkness shifted around her.

She thought she heard her name. Not spoken by voice but by the whisper of the trees and the hiss of the wind. The syllables running through her blood.

Melody...come...come...come...back...

She took another step. The trees closed in, their trunks pale in the thin light. Something moved ahead of her. She froze.

The shape lingered in the dark between trees. A breath. A shadow heavier than the   others. The hat is low. The faint gleam where eyes should have been.

Her heart stuttered. The mark on her arm flared like heat. She opened her mouth, but no sound came. Then a branch cracked behind her.

She turned, startled.

"Mel?"

His chest rose and fell like he'd been running. His hair was wet from mist, his clothes rumpled. The flashlight in his hand trembled, its beam cutting through her. The light caught her face, her eyes wide and vacant, the pallor of her skin almost silver. He took a step forward, calling her name, but she didn't move.

She stood like someone waking from a long dream. Then his gaze dropped.

Her sleeve had slipped down. The bean caught the bruises on her shoulder, the marks winding down her arm like dark vines. Some old, some fresh.

Vince's face changed. The breath left him in a shudder. His mouth opened but no sound came. The light trembled harder. He took another step, slow, as though approaching something that might vanish.

She looked at him, her eyes hollow, reflecting the beam of his flashlight.

For a moment they were both silent. The forest around them held its breath. The trees leaned inward, their branches whispering. He reached out a hand. She didn't take it. The light flickered. Between them, the dark seemed to move—not away, but closer. The space itself bends.

Vince's face broke open with fear. Not of her. Not entirely. Of what stood just beyond her shoulder, unseen except in the tremor of the air.

The flashlight slipped from his hand and fell into the leaves.

"It's happening again," he said. "My brother, Casey. Now you," he added.

The beam of light rolled sideways, carving strange shapes against the trunks.

"I'm not going to let it." He stepped forward. Melody took a step back. Above them the branches shook, though there was no wind. "I'm not going to let you disappear."

He lunged forward and took her in his arms. The warmth of his body pressed against her face. It pulled her back into the world with a start. One that made her cry. He held her as she sobbed. In the faint distance, deeper in the woods, something began to hum—a sound too low, too steady, to belong to anything human.

9

MUSIC TO THE EARS

T he world opened in flame.

A red wind moved across the fields, and the ground steamed beneath. Every tree was ash, and the sky burned low as if it had been set too near the earth. Melody stood at the edge of a garden that glowed like iron left in a forge, each flower a coal pulsing from within.

The air shuddered.

The smell was metal and dust.

She heard the wings before she saw them. A long, slow beat that stirred the smoke into spirals. Then a shriek.

The Eggstabletman came down through the haze, the gray of him almost silver in that light, his rags drawn wide like a cloak. Behind him spread shapes that might have been wings, or the mere memory of wings. Great folds of darkness that caught the heat and flung it back her way.

He landed without a sound. The earth sank under him.

She ran. The soil clung to her shoes. Hot and soft.

The air itself seemed to clutch at her arms. When she turned, he was already there—closer, impossibly so—his head bent, his face hidden beneath the brim.

He moved. The wings came round her, the wind of them sharp enough to cut. Her hair whipped across her eyes. He struck. A flash of movement, a blow that carried the weight of stone. She fell hard into the burning grass. The world dimmed.

He leaned over her, the shadow of him shaking with the pulse of burning heat. Something touched her shoulder, and she felt the world narrow to that single point of pain, deep and searing, as if a brand had been pressed into her flesh. The smell of her own fear filled her mouth. But all for nothing. His mouth tore at her flesh. It ripped it clean off the bone. Tendons snapped and squelched in his mouth as he chewed, blood dripping from his jowls.

The Eggstabletman came in again. Melody lashed out, her other hand finding the ground, closing around a shard of blackened stone. She swung blind. The shard met resistance. A sound like wet fabric tearing.

He recoiled. His head twisted. His wings fanned out as he began to screech. A hiss followed, low and long.

She crawled to her feet. Her arm hung useless, blood dripping down it. But she faced him. He rose to his full height, taller than before, the firelight sliding down the length of him. The wings spread wide again, edges glinting. He came forward.

She struck once more, and the shard vanished into him, swallowed by the rags.

A sound broke the air. Another shriek. Guttural and tormented. The Eggstabletman staggered.

The wings shuddered, folding in upon themselves, and then they were gone, drawn back into the gray body like smoke returning to its source.

The garden burned quieter now. He stood for a moment, trembling. The brim of his hat lifted enough that she could see the emptiness beneath it, a hollow that shimmered with red light. Then he turned away, fading into the fumes, and the fire dimmed with him.

Melody fell to her knees. Her body shook. She tried to reach for her shoulder, but it was not there. The skin around it was hot and raw. The smell of ash and blood hung in the air, and somewhere above, the wings beat once, twice, and were gone.

She stayed there a long time, in the heat and silence, her breath the only living sound in the world that remained.

The seasons passed without her noticing. The years no longer arranged themselves clearly in Melody's mind. The months bled together, the weather changing without meaning. Somewhere along the way she had frozen her classes. No one knew. The school still sent emails that went unanswered. The world, she had found, would let you vanish if you only stood still.

Her room had grown different. Not unkempt, not entirely, but still. Dust gathered on the desk where her books once lay open. The curtains were seldom drawn. Light came through in thin threads that fell across the floor like old rope. The air smelled faintly of paper and too much sleep.

Vince came by sometimes. She let him in now. He never asked about the classes. Perhaps he knew. Perhaps he understood that there are things you cannot ask without undoing what little remains.

They would talk. Not always much. He would sit on the floor with his back to the wall, guitar across his lap, and she would sit on the edge of the bed, legs folded under her. He played quietly, nothing whole, just threads of songs that hung in the air between them. Sometimes she hummed without realising. When he stopped, she looked at him as if waking from somewhere far away.

He still went out each night to search for Casey, but he didn't tell her much about it. What he spoke of was the world outside. A place she didn't seem to want to be part of anymore. Each time he did, her eyes drifted elsewhere. Behind them, something moved. Not seen but felt. A presence that lived in the space between his words.

When she spoke, it was of dancing. Her voice changed with it. Softer, steadier. She told him how it used to feel, the weightlessness, the sense that the body was only the echo of something larger. But her hands trembled when she described it, and once he caught her staring at the corner of the room, lips moving, whispering to someone not there.

He asked what she'd said. She shook her head. "Nothing."

On the table by the window lay a small notebook. Its pages were filled with sketches. Shapes of motion, half-drawn figures, lines that spiralled and broke apart. He picked it up once, and she flinched. He never did it again.

They took walks sometimes. Short ones. She moved slowly, her limp more pronounced now, her body slight in the cold air. He'd talk to fill the silence. About the book he was reading, about a new song he wanted to finish. She would listen, her gaze fixed somewhere just beyond the horizon. The trees along the path leaned toward her as she passed, or maybe it only seemed so.

Once, on a late afternoon walk, the light broke thinly through the clouds, she said. "Do you ever think we live in two places at once?"

Vince frowned. "What do you mean?"

"Like maybe we're walking here," she said, "but some part of us is somewhere else. Following the same steps."

He didn't answer. The wind moved through the trees and she smiled faintly.

"I'm only kidding," she said.

When they returned to her room, he helped her tidy the space. He straightened the sheets, gathered the empty mugs, and opened the curtains. She thanked him softly, her voice smaller than the sound of the wind outside. He sat again with the guitar and played until dusk came.

She watched him. The music filled the room, gentle, imperfect. It should have been peaceful. But something in her face told him it wasn't. The darkness lived there still, deep behind the eyes, coiled and patient. It had not left her. Only waited.

He caught her looking past him again, toward the shadowed corner where the light failed to reach. Her lips moved. He couldn't hear the words, but he knew she wasn't speaking to him.

He stopped playing. The strings' last note trembled and died. When she looked back, her face was calm again. "Play another," she said.

He did. Because what else was there to do? The music rose once more, quiet and fragile. Like breath on glass. The dark held still for a time, listening. She looked on towards it. In that corner. It swayed, gently, in tune with the music. Its shape grew. It became tangible. She could see the rags and the edges of the hat. Melody drew back a moment but stared on. He watched her. Vince or *him*? Who was singing? She could not tell anymore. It did not matter. She listened. Hummed. And she swayed. She would've liked to dance, but she didn't have the strength anymore. She closed her eyes so she could not see. Only listen. It was a soothing song. One that took her away. Far, far away. Somewhere warm and comforting. Where things made sense.

The music stopped.

"Have you thought of visiting home?"

Melody didn't open her eyes. She tried to decipher whose voice she was hearing.

"No," she said. Still searching. "I haven't. Why?"

"It might be a good idea. Fewer people around."

"Hmmm..."

"You don't think so?"

"Are you trying to get rid of me?" she asked.

"Don't be ridiculous. You know I'm not."

"Then?"

He hesitated. "I'm just scared I might lose you."

"Who do you think I am?"

"I don't know," he said. "I really don't, Mel. One moment you're here, and then you're not. I want you, Melody."

"You want me?"

"Yes. I want you."

A faint smile crossed her lips. "Going home wouldn't help with that."

"It will. You would be safe."

"Safe?" she asked. "From what?"

"From *him*."

Melody opened her eyes. The room was silent. Vince sat with his back to the wall, a frown on his face as he looked directly at her.

"You, okay?" he asked.

"Yes," she smiled. "I was just thinking."

"What about?"

"You," she said. "About what you said."

Melody slipped off the bed. She kneeled and went close to him. Vince lifted his guitar, as if in defense.

"What are you doing, Mel?"

"Nothing," she said, placing her hand on his face. "I'm doing nothing." She caressed him. Held his warmth in her palm. "I like you, Vince. I like you a lot."

"I—I like you t-too, Mel. But—"

"No, please," she hushed him. "No buts."

"Mel..."He drew back. "It's not right."

She looked at him as if he was another. "Why not? You said you want me."

"What?"

"You said you want me, Vince. I want you, too. Please." She dragged herself towards him. He picked up his guitar and stood. "Don't leave. I just want to be with you."

"I don't want to leave, Mel, but you're making me uncomfortable."

Melody stiffened. "Leave now," she said, "and you'll have another Casey on your hands. Is that what you want? For me to go missing like her? Like your brother?"

"Mel—what the fuck? Why would you say that?"

"I need you, Vince. I need you now more than ever. Please." Tears trickled down her face. "Have me."

"This is too much," he said, shaking his head. "You're doing too much. Look," he sighed. "I know you're going through something. We both are. But please, Mel. Don't force things. Don't make things awkward. It's too soon. I still...I still—"

"Screw her!" she shouted. "Screw Casey! I was first!" She stood up. Stumbled and fell. Hit hard against the floor.

"Mel!"

"I can dance!" She tried again. Fell once more. "I can dance, Vince! You like it when I dance. Is that why? Because I haven't been—look," she forced herself to her feet. Her leg had gone bad again, or so it seemed. She forced herself to stand. To move and spin like she once did. "Look," she strained herself to smile. "You can play the guitar and—and I—I can—"

She fell hard against the floor.

"Jesus Christ, Mel." His eyes glanced towards the desk. He went and took her phone and left the room, closing the door behind him. The room had gone still without him.

His words hung in the air long after the door closed, as if they had weight enough to stay when he could not. The sound of his footsteps in the hall faded slowly, then nothing.

Her hands trembled in her lap. Time came apart in the dark. One second her face was dry, the next, completely wet. Her throat was raw. The sobs came soundless. There was only the shake of her shoulders.

He returned without a word. He placed the phone back down on the desk and then sat on the bed.

"I called your parents," he said. "They're on their way."

The world ripped apart. She cried in mourning for a life that she had barely been able to graze with her fingertips. It felt real and whole nonetheless and now it was getting taken away from her.

It must have been hours. Because the knocks came. The voices. A woman's. Soft and breaking. A man's, low and careful and sincere. Her mother stood in the doorway, face pale, eyes wide, her hand covering her mouth.

Behind her, Victor. He stood only a moment before he ran in and held her in his arms. He kissed her head. He whispered words that did not reach her. He looked up at the man sitting on the edge of the bed.

"Who are you?"

Vince looked to the mother.

"He's the one that called," she said. "The friend."

Victor nodded.

The mother came, too, and knelt. They held her close and tried to press her into the girl they once knew, even though it was clear that no matter how hard they were to try, they would never succeed.

"Let's go home, Mel," her father said. "You'll be better off there."

10

BACK WHERE ONE BELONGS

It all began in snow that was not snow. It fell soundless and heavy, gray against the dark. When it touched her, it melted into thin trails of ash. The ground beneath her feet was neither earth nor ice but something that shifted with breath, as if the world itself were drawing her down into its lungs.

She stood barefoot. The cold bit at her bones. Her reflection gleamed faintly in the ice crust at her feet. Then the light changed. The air took on weight.

He came from the distance as he always did, first a smudge in the pale, then a figure walking through a storm that bent to let him pass.

She had no weapon. Her arms hung at her sides, the flesh recovered.

The wind grew sharper as he drew near. She saw the wings behind him, no longer the shadowed half-things of before but whole and immense, their edges catching what little light there was. They stretched outward like walls, folding the horizon closed. The snow swirled in circles around him, caught in the updraft of their slow beating.

He raised his head. The light struck beneath the brim, and she saw nothing but the void of his face, as if every feature had been swallowed by its own shadow. The whisper came like breath over glass.

"I have waited," he said.

The wings unfurled fully, blotting out the sky. The ground broke beneath her, thin plates of ice fracturing, a white sea opening its jaws. She fell to her knees, the cold biting her palms. When she looked up, he was already upon her.

The air cracked. The wind carried the smell of earth long buried. His hand closed on her shoulder, and she felt the press of nails through skin, the weight of something ancient and tireless. He lifted her as if she weighed nothing, the wings beating once, raising them both above the ground.

The world below was endless white. Her heart thundered in her chest.

Then he struck.

It was not a blow but a fall. They cracked through the air, spinning. The ice rose to meet them like a mirror shattering. She hit the ground hard enough to feel the bones in her back squeal. The light dimmed, the wings folding around them both like a shroud.

He leaned close. His breath was a sound like wind through a grave. The brim of his hat brushed her cheek. She could not move. The cold in his touch seeped through her flesh, a tide that froze thought itself.

He whispered, and the words coiled through her like smoke.

"Long enough. Too many years."

Then came the pain. Sharp, consuming, unseen. Her back arched under it. The sound that left her was not quite a scream.

The wings trembled. His shadow filled the world as he shuddered, feeding.

But something in her moved still. The pulse within her chest rose like a drumbeat. She remembered the rhythm, the steps she'd danced alone in her room, the motion that had once freed her from fear. Her body turned despite the pain. Even as her flesh got torn apart by his mouth, her hand struck upward, fingers finding the edge of his coat. She twisted, dragging him with her, using the fall itself as her strength.

The ground split open beneath them. A lightning burst through the ice. Not white, but gold, a color too bright to hold.

He reeled back, the wings flaring, the word behind his hidden face flickering. She pushed herself to her feet, unsteady, bleeding from the unseen wound that seared her side. He staggered, hat tipping, one hand clutching the air as though it were slipping from him.

For a moment the world stilled. The snow hung motionless. The air burned clean.

Then he was gone.

The wings folded inward and collapsed into smoke. The wind died. Only the silence remained, thick and endless.

She stood there shaking, her hands slick with the cold that was not water, her breath tearing at her throat.

When she looked down, she saw her reflection once more in the fractured ice. Her own eyes staring up at her, wide and pale, a shadow moving just behind them.

And the whisper came faintly, as if from under the world itself:

Next time, little dancer. Next time we finish it.

The house was small and grew smaller by the day. The year had folded itself into sameness. The days moved like the slow turn of a wheel sunk deep in mud. The light came and went and meant nothing. The trees beyond the house stood bare, their branches black against a pale sky, and in their stillness, there was something that resembled peace, though it was not peace at all.

Melody stayed in the front room now. The walls were painted the color of cream, but the corners had yellowed where the light seldom reached.

The window looked out onto the yard and the line of woods beyond. Her wheelchair sat there beside the glass, always angled toward the world outside, as if she might at any moment decide to join it. She never did.

Her mother moved quietly around her. The sound of dishes from the kitchen, the smell of bread, the rustle of fabric as she folded clothes. Sometimes she hummed without realising it, old hymns that had lost their meaning in the long years between. She tried to talk to Melody, to draw her back with gentle words. *What would you like for breakfast, honey? You want to go for a little walk?* The voice was kind but distant, directed toward someone who no longer lived here.

Her father came and went with the seasons. He worked the land as he always had. When the ground was hard with frost, he mended the fences, split wood, and cleared snow from the drive. She watched him through the window as if he were a stranger. He'd turn to wave at her, a smile on his face. She never could return the favor.

Victor spoke less than her mother, but his silence was heavy with all the things that he could've and should've said. He would stand sometimes at the door, watching Melody in her chair, and she would turn and meet his eyes, and that was enough to fill the room with ache.

She had grown thinner. The skin along her arms was pale—where she wasn't bruised— and drawn tight over the bone. Her hair hung dull around her face, unkempt, as if she had forgotten it belonged to her.

She returned to the wheelchair. It had, once more, become an extension of her body, the metal cold beneath her fingers. Her legs seldom moved. Her hands shook when she lifted them.

The doctors said it was exhaustion. They talked about nutrition, of medicine. Of other things she did not want to think about. Her parents nodded along with it all, hoping that somewhere along the way, it would all work out.

Her mother took her into town once a week, pushing the chair through the park. The ducks moved slowly across the pond, the wind lifting the reeds. Children laughed on the far side of the water. Melody sat without speaking, her gaze following the shifting light on the surface. When her mother asked what she was thinking, she said nothing. Her lips barely moved.

At home, her father wheeled her down the path to the woods when the evenings were warm enough. He told her the names of the trees, pointed to tracks in the dirt, to a hawk turning high above. She listened, her head tilted as though hearing something between his words. She smiled faintly, not at what he said, but at the odd shapes scratched into her vision bending around each trunk.

The bruises darkened, spreading along her shoulders, her ribs, her arms. Her mother found them when she bathed her and wept in silence, turning her face away so Melody would not see. When she asked how they happened, Melody only said she didn't remember. But the marks came, again and again. Cold to the touch.

She began to murmur at night. Words her parents could not make out, soft and rhythmic, almost like prayer. Her father would stand in the hall listening until her voice faded into the creak of the old boards. Then he would go back to bed and lie awake beside his wife, both of them staring at the ceiling until dawn.

They bought her a small radio to fill the silence. She toyed with it on the first day and hummed along and gave them hope. She left it off from then on. The quiet suited her better.

When summer came and Ford came home from college, Melody realised that he had not been there that entire time. Perhaps she had been distracted by the golden fields or her father tending to them.

Ford was thin and sun-browned. His hair is longer, a paint stain on the cuff of his shirt. He carried sketchbooks under one arm and hugged India as if afraid she might vanish when he let go. He spoke quickly, full of the city and its noise, of professors who argued about color and of the friends he made and missed already. He laughed often and threw quick glances at her. But never something committed and honest. As if he was afraid.

A week later, Baller came back. He had filled out, his face harder, his beard rough along his jaw. He smelled faintly of metal and the sterile air of laboratories. His mind moved the way their father's hands once had— deliberate, certain.

That first night they all ate together at the big table. The fans turned slow above them. The window screens clicked with moths. Their mother had cooked too much—roast chicken, sweet corn, potatoes slick with butter. Their father sat at the head of the table as always, looking between them, not knowing what mask to draw over his face.

Melody sat at the far end, her wheelchair drawn close to the table. The light from the window fell across her arms, pale and thin as candle wax. She smiled when spoken to, but her eyes drifted beyond the faces, toward the trees visible through the glass. The sun caught in her hair. Her hands rested motionless in her lap.

Ford tried to draw her in. "You'd like the school, Mel," he said. "They've got dancers there, too. A whole studio of them."

Her lips parted. "Do they have singers?"

"Singers?" Ford threw a quick glance towards his parents. "Sure, they have singers."

"Do they sing nice?"

"Well..." He hesitated. "I never heard them myself, so I wouldn't know. But I'm told they're good."

"That's nice."

An awkward tension crept into the whole table. Ford reached across the table. "We'll take you outside tomorrow," he said. "You can sit in the garden while I draw."

Melody met his eyes and smiled, a small tremor of light that faded almost as soon as it appeared.

The talk turned again. Baller told a story about the university. An experiment that went wrong. There was little interest. Her mother cared more about all the disappearances she kept on hearing about. The conversation went nowhere, and the rest was spent in absolute silence.

The following day they did as Ford had suggested.

The noon light lay hard on the garden. Heat shimmered above the soil beds, the air humming with insects. Baller had dragged two old chairs out beneath the elm and set them near where Melody's wheelchair rested. Ford sat cross-legged in the grass with his sketchbook open on his knees, a pencil darkening the page in slow strokes.

"So, college," Baller coughed. "Any girls catch your eye, Fordie?"

"Shut up." He flushed.

"I'll take that as a yes. Wouldn't you, Mel?" He turned to her. She couldn't even smile. "What about you? Any guys lucky enough to catch your interest?"

"There's one," she said softly.

"Yeah?"

Melody nodded. "He's not from here, though."

"You'd hope not. Nothing good ever comes from this place," he spat, "except for this family, of course."

"Nice save, man." Ford chuckled.

The younger brother would lift his head and watch Melody as he drew. At first the lines came easy—the tilt of her head, the fall of her dress, the long shadow of the chair across the grass. Then something began to change. The pencil moved of its own accord. Shapes formed at the edge of the paper, faint and wrong. The shadows deepened where he hadn't pressed. A darkness leaking outward. He frowned, tried to erase, but the marks remained. They thickened, joined, became the outline of a figure standing behind her. The shape of a hat. The curve of the hands is too long.

"What's with that look?" Baller turned to him.

"Nothing," Ford said. He shut the book halfway, but Melody had already turned toward him. Her eyes met his. A smile on her face. "It's just not that good."

"Let me see," she said.

"It's not finished."

"You artists and your shyness," Baller spat. "Come on. Let the girl see."

Ford shook his head. "I can't. Out of principle."

Melody tilted her head. "It's behind me, isn't it?"

"What?" Baller frowned.

Her gaze held her younger brother. "A figure with a brimmed hat," she said. "That's what you have drawn, right? Long claws. Rags falling down its body. You see it, too, Fordie?"

"What are you talking about?" Baller looked between the two. "Fordie. Is that what you drew?"

"Well—"

"Show me that."

Baller jumped from his seat and ripped the book from Ford's hands. He opened it and landed directly on the drawing of her.

He looked up at her. "Mel...how did you know that?"

She didn't answer. Her eyes grew heavy. A thin tremor passed through her shoulders.

"Mel?" Baller called. "Mel, what's wrong?"

"He..." She muttered. "He doesn't like the light."

Melody closed her eyes. In the darkness, she slumped.

11

THE OTHER SIDE

She drifted in darkness.

The water held her as if she weighed nothing; a wide plain of liquid night stretching to no horizon. No sky above, only more dark, the air thick as oil. The water beneath her rocked with the slow pulse of something breathing far below.

She did not know how long she had been there. Time dissolved in the current. She tried to lift her hand, but the effort felt distant, as though her body belonged to another dreamer somewhere else.

Beneath her, shapes moved. She saw them dimly through the dark. The outline of streets, the glimmer of windows, the small pulse of lamps. A town—her town—whole and sunken, resting quiet at the bottom of this dark sea. The church steeple jutted upward like a bone through deep-blue flesh. It was odd. It resembled home and yet it had the characteristic of an *otherness* about it. As though something imperceptible to the eye had been changed about the very walls of the buildings.

People drifted among the rooftops, lifeless, their faces turned upward as if waiting for something to fall.

She called out, but her voice was swallowed before it left her throat. The sound became a ripple spreading across the surface and vanishing.

The raft rocked. She felt the weight of eyes beneath her. Not many, but one pair. Vast and patient. Watching from somewhere deep.

The current turned. The town below shifted. The houses broke apart like paper left too long in the rain. The people drifted from the streets and rose toward her, their limbs pale ribbons, their bodies bloated and drowned. She saw faces she knew: her mother, her father, her brothers. The young girl who went missing. The boy that shot her. They floated just beneath the raft, mouths opening and closing as if speaking through water. The sound was gone, but she understood the words all the same:

Come down. It's quiet here.

Melody looked up instead. The sky was a single black sheet. No stars. No wind. Only the endless reflection of herself, staring back from the surface above. Two worlds of dark, mirrored and indistinguishable.

The raft began to tilt. A slow lean at first, then sharper. The water licked her arm, cold and alive. She pressed her palms flat against the boards, but the motion would not stop. Something beneath had a hold of the raft.

The town lights flickered to the colour of his eyes. The faces turned to that dark red hue. Then the dead eyes opened. Small and red, all of them. Looking right at her.

She felt their pull. Deep. Steady. Not a hand. Not claws. A summons. The same gravity that had followed her through every dream.

The raft shuddered. The boards cracked. She could taste the salt on her lips.

The whisper rose through the water, soft as breath.

"Little dancer, the time is near. You float too much; you must come here."

A clawed hand broke through to the surface. It reached for her. Melody closed her eyes and let the raft go. For a heartbeat, she hung between water and air, between waking and the long descent.

Then she fell.

And the ocean closed over her like a curtain drawn.

She woke up to heat. It clung to her like a second skin, thick and damp, seeping through the sheets. The world came to her in pieces: the ceiling above, the shadowed blur of figures moving in the room, the sound of her own breath, shallow and quick. She tried to speak and could not. Her throat burned dry.

Her body shivered though the air was heavy with warmth. Sweat slid down her temples and pooled in the hollow of her throat. She could not tell if she was awake or still drifting in the black ocean. The dream had not ended so much as thinned, its edges leaking through.

Voices came from somewhere nearby. Muffled, uncertain. A hand touched her arm, and she flinched!

"It's me," Baller said. "It's just me."

She turned her head slightly. He sat beside the bed, his chair pulled close, his face pale and drawn tight. One of his hands held hers, the other rested on the edge of the mattress. She felt the tremor in his grip. He had not slept.

The door opened. Light from the hallway spilled across the floor. India entered, carrying two bowls of steaming water. The scent of it filled the air. Herbs and salt and the faint metallic note of the well. She set them on the nightstand and dipped a cloth into one, wringing it out before laying it across Melody's forehead.

"You poor thing," she said softly.

Baller stared at the small bruises along Melody's arms, at the marks that had never fully faded.

Ford sat near the window. His sketchbook lay closed on the sill. He hadn't touched it since the incident in the garden. The light coming through the glass drew a pale square across the floor. Dust turned in it like slow snow. He watched the light instead of her.

Melody shifted under the sheets. Her body jerked once, then again, her breath catching in short, startled bursts. Her mother placed another cloth on her chest. Steam rose from the bowl. The room smelled of heat and worry.

Victor stood in the doorway. He filled it completely. His hands hung loose at his sides. He said nothing. His eyes stayed fixed on his daughter, not with fear but with something heavier. A resignation that had no name.

"Should we call the doctor?" Ford asked quietly.

His mother shook her head. "He can't do anything the Lord hasn't already tried."

Ford's gaze dropped. He looked at Baller, but his brother's expression offered no comfort. His composure had broken. Beneath it lived a boy who did not know what to do.

Melody stirred again. Her eyes opened halfway, glassy and unfocused. She mumbled something. The words blurred, barely formed. Baller leaned closer.

"What is it, Mel?"

Her lips moved. "They're...they're under the water," she whispered.

Baller swallowed hard. "Who is?"

Her voice faded. The next sound from her mouth was not speech but a low hum, soft and rhythmic, like a lullaby.

India dipped another cloth, replaced the one on her forehead, smoothed the hair from her face. "Hush now," she said. "It's just a fever dream."

The air in the room thickened. Outside, thunder rolled in the distance. The sky was darkening toward rain.

Ford stood, restless. He crossed to the window and looked out at the yard, the trees moving slowly in the wind. He thought of the figure he had drawn. For a moment, it seemed as though it stood out there now, among the trees, waiting.

Behind him, Melody gasped. The sound was sharp, breaking the stillness. Her back arched, her fingers clawed at the sheets. Baller held her shoulders, whispering her name. Her eyes were closed tight, her face twisted in some private terror. The fever glowed through her skin.

"Easy," he said. "You're safe here."

But she was not here with them. Her voice came again, disjointed, a language half-dreamt. "It's calling," she murmured. "From below."

India began to pray under her breath. The words blurred together, soft and urgent.

Victor finally moved. He stepped into the room and stood at the foot of the bed, his hands gripping the frame. The wood creaked under his weight.

"Melody," he said, his voice rough. "You fight it, you hear? You fight it."

She did not answer.

The rain started then. A thin patter at first, then steady, drumming against the roof. The sound filled the spaces between their words. The light in the room dimmed to amber.

Ford went to fetch more water but stopped at the doorway. His father's eyes met his. Two men with no language for what they saw. He turned back to the bed and watched his sister breathing shallowly, the sheets damp with sweat. He thought she looked like something caught between worlds.

Her mother replaced the cloth again. Baller never let go of her arm. He kept counting her pulse under his breath, though he no longer trusted the rhythm. It came uneven, fading and returning, like the tide she'd once dreamed about.

She whispered once more, barely audible: "He's near."

The words fell into the rain.

Her mother didn't hear or pretended not to. She straightened the blanket, wiped Melody's hands.

"Rest now, darling. Just rest."

The storm grew louder. Electricity flickered, then steadied. Victor stepped back into the doorway again and leaned his shoulder against the frame. His head bowed slightly, eyes closed. He looked like a man listening for a sound he hoped not to hear.

Hours passed. The bowls cooled. The clothes dried. The room held the smell of sweat and rain and something faintly gone.

Near midnight, Melody stilled. Her breathing eased, her body slackened. Her mother's shoulders sagged with relief. "There," she whispered. "There now."

Baller kept his hand on her wrist. Her pulse beat faintly against his fingers, not gone, but changed.

Outside, the rain slowed. The trees gleamed black in the lightning's brief light. Somewhere in the woods, an owl cried and fell silent.

The storm had passed. The house was quiet again, emptied of sound except for the small, steady crackle of the candle on the nightstand. The wick spat and leaned in the draft, its flame fluttering against the dark. Baller sat beside the bed, his shoulders bent, the collar of his shirt damp with sweat. He had opened the window to let the heat out but the air that came in was no cooler, only heavy with the smell of wet soil and rain.

Melody lay half-turned on her side, her face slick with fever still. Her breathing came shallow and slow. The light from the candle trembled across her skin, the shadows moving like water over her. Her eyes were open but clouded, fixed on some point that wasn't there.

Baller watched her as he had for hours. Every movement of her chest felt counted, borrowed. When she stirred, he leaned forward, touching her hand gently, whispering her name. She blinked but didn't answer. She was fighting sleep. He could see the tremor in her eyelids, the way she kept forcing them open.

"Mel," he said, "you should rest."

Her lips moved but the words that came were thin. "No. I...I can't. Not again."

He frowned. "What do you mean?"

"He waits when I sleep."

The room breathed in silence. The candle popped. He glanced towards the window. Beyond it, the night.

"It's just the fever," he said, yet his voice lacked conviction

She stared at him, pupils wide, her gaze so full of terror it hollowed him.

"Don't let me sleep," she whispered. "Promise."

He hesitated. "All right," he said. "I'll stay awake with you."

She closed her eyes briefly, then opened them again as though waking from a deeper place.

"You can't keep him out."

Baller reached for the cloth on her forehead, dipped it in the bowl, wrung it out. He pressed the cool water to her skin. "I will," he said, not understanding. "Don't worry."

But she was already slipping. Her gaze unfocused, her mouth twitching faintly. The shadows in the corners of the room began to deepen. He dabbed at his eyes, tired, and when he looked again, something had shifted. The light of the candle had grown dimmer, its flame guttering in a sudden breath of air that hadn't come from the open window.

He straightened. "Mel?"

She looked at him. For a moment, her eyes cleared, and what he saw in them froze him.

Her breath hitched. Her lips trembled. "No," she whispered. "No, not you. Go away."

He reached for her hand, but she recoiled weakly, the motion slight but sharp. Tears welled in her eyes.

"Mel—what's wrong?"

She began to sob. Quiet and broken. "Leave me alone. I...I don't want to go. Let me stay. Let me..."

The words fell between them like ash. He stared at her, stunned, the candlelight painting him in long shadows. "It's me," he said. "It's Baller."

But her gaze was fixed somewhere else now, not at him, but through him. Her expression twisted, fear collapsing into despair.

"At least..." she whispered. "Take off the hat."

He looked down at himself, at his bare head, his plain shirt, his hands trembling. The flame jumped again, long and thin, and in the wall's reflection, he saw something move. A darker shape superimposed over his own.

Baller froze. His pulse thudded heavy in his ears. He turned back to her. Her eyes followed him, wide and glassy.

"Don't...don't come closer."

He stepped back. "Mel, you're dreaming."

"You...you...stay away!"

Her voice rose into a sobbing shrill. He wanted to reach for her again, to hold her, but he could not make himself move. The candlelight flared, throwing his shadow huge and bent across the wall. For an instant, it did not look like his own. The shoulders hunched, the arms too long. Fingers stretched thin as branches.

He turned, breathed unsteady, and pressed his palms to his face. His mind screamed at him that it was only the light, that the candle was low, that shadows always lied. But still, he could feel something behind the illusion.

Melody's sobs softened. She was fading, sinking back toward sleep despite herself. Her head rolled to the side. The fever's sheen on her skin looked like water catching light. Her lips moved without sound.

"Mel..." he called.

But she could no longer hear him. Her eyes fluttered once, twice, then closed completely. Her breathing deepened. The tears still clung to her lashes.

Baller stood frozen beside the bed. The room seemed to hold its breath. The candle flickered, its light guttering low, and for a heartbeat, he thought he saw someone else standing where he stood.

He staggered back until his legs struck the wall. His hand brushed against the window frame, and cold air flooded in. The vision broke. The candle steadied. It was only him again.

He looked at Melody. She was still, now. The fever had eased but her face was pale, her lips parted slightly. Her chest rose and fell with a slow rhythm. He knelt beside the bed and whispered her name, but she did not answer. Her fingers twitched once, then went still again.

He could not tell if she slept or dreamed or had fallen somewhere in between. The air around her seemed thicker, as if the room itself leaned closer to listen.

The candle burned lower. Wax dripped down the side of the table, hardening into pale rivers. Outside, the insects had gone quiet. The house made no sound.

Baller sat back in his chair, the exhaustion closing over him like a wave. He watched her breathing. Watched the small tremors that passed through her body. Watched the faint movement beneath her eyelids, the trace of a dream she could not escape.

"You're better off," he said. "Sleep is what you need."

Yet as he said it, he had doubts that it was true. Whatever held her now was beyond his reach.

The candlelight flickered once more and went out.

In the dark, Baller thought he heard her whisper something back. A name. Or a prayer. Or the soft hum of a lullaby that he did not recognize.

Then there was nothing at all.

12

THE WOODS

The sky was a bruise. Purple and black, stretched thin above a field of fire. The smell of smoke filled her lungs before she opened her eyes. When she did, she found herself standing in the ash. The world around her burned. A carnival undone, its tents aflame, the fabric curling like dying skin.

The wind carried music, distant and warped, a calliope playing from nowhere. She turned and saw the striped peaks of the circus melting into the horizon, their colors running like blood in water. The ground trembled beneath her feet. Mirrors lay shattered across the earth, glinting with flame. In them, she saw reflections that weren't her own.

The shadows whispered. They swayed where the light met the smoke, bending like tall grass in invisible wind. Each voice was familiar, the echo of something lost.

She stood barefoot, the ash sticking to her soles. Her body was no longer weak, her legs straight and certain beneath her. The air rippled. The music slowed. And then he came.

The Eggstabletman stepped from the blaze. His hat was pulled low, the rim blackened by soot. His rags hung in tatters, their edges aflame. His face was almost human now, its hollowness filled with light from the burning tents. The eyes beneath the brim glowed red, small and sharp as coals. He was smiling.

"The time has come," he said.

"For it to end," she replied.

He tilted his head, the movement graceful, almost kind. Smoke curled through the holes of his form. He raised one clawed hand, and the shadows behind him rose with it. Silhouettes of men and beasts and things without names. They whispered her name like a prayer.

Melody bent and lifted a shard of mirror from the ground. Its edge was jagged, its surface smeared with ash. She could see his reflection in it, taller, broader, less human. She could see herself too. Gaunt. Her eyes alight with fever and resolve.

He moved first. A blur through flame. The air hissed where his claws struck. She ducked, felt the heat pass over her, the ash rose like smoke around her. The ground broke open under his step, a deep sound like thunder. She swung the mirror shard, and it caught the side of his arm, cutting black smoke that bled like ink.

He hissed, soft and low.

"Remember who taught you how to dance."

She stepped back, breath ragged. The ground shifted, the circus tents collapsing in waves, their poles snapping like bones. Fire spilled into the sea that surrounded them, the water below black and gleaming. The whole place floated on it. The circus, the battlefield, the world.

He lunged again. This time she didn't retreat. She spun, let his momentum pass her, drove the shard deep into the hollow where his chest should have been. The sound it made was not of tearing flesh but breaking glass. The mirrors across the ground all shattered at once, their surfaces erupting in a chorus of screams.

The Eggstabletman staggered. His body split with light, crimson at first, then white, the brilliance of something ancient and dying. He reached for her. The touch of his fingers against her cheek was almost gentle.

"You...you will miss me," he whispered.

Then he fell. His body dissolved into smoke, the hat tumbling last, rolling once across the ash before sliding into the sea. The waves swallowed it whole.

Melody stood alone. The circus burned lower. The wind stilled. The music faded into nothing. She looked down at her hands. Bloodless. Shaking. The mirror shard had melted to nothing, leaving only the faint sting of heat in her palm.

She exhaled, slow. "It's over."

The words vanished into the vastness. She could hear the sea below, the slow churn of it against the wreckage. She walked to the edge of the broken pier that jutted from the ruins of the circus. Beyond it was only darkness.

She should have woken then. She waited for it. The feeling of being pulled upward, the sudden rush of breath, the weight of sheets and gravity. But nothing came. The air stayed heavy. The fire burned on. The dream did not end.

Panic rose in her throat. She pressed her hands to her face, her body trembling.

"I...I shouldn't be here. I...Baller...Mom...Dad...Ford...Bring me home. Wake up! Come on! I beat him! I killed him! I—"

She turned in circles, calling for them all. Only echoes answered. Thin voices threading through the wreckage. She took a step toward them, but the ground beneath her foot gave way. The wood of the pier split, the boards sagging. She dropped to her knees and looked down.

The black water shifted. Beneath its surface, shapes moved. Slow and immense. Eyes opened there, hundreds of them, small and red like distant dying suns beneath the tide. The water rippled with their motion, each glimmering form distinct, yet each wearing the same hat, the same rags, the same long and reaching hands.

She stumbled back, but the pier ended behind her. The air thinned. The sea began to rise. The voices that had once called her name now chanted it, low and pulse-like, the sound of a thousand whispers breathing as one. The surface broke. One of the figures began to climb out. An Eggstabletman, whole again, his face glistening with the reflection of the burning sky. Behind him came more, endless.

"No!" she breathed. "You're gone!"

But they were not. They had never been gone.

The pier broke entirely. She fell. The water closed above her head. Cold seized her body like hands. The light of the fire refracted in the depths, turning red, then gold, then black. All around her, the creatures moved, slow and vast, their hats drifting like dark stars.

She tried to scream, but the water filled her mouth. Her eyes burned. She kicked upward but there was no surface, only more depth. The whispers surrounded her, echoing inside her skull until they were indistinguishable from her own thoughts.

Her limbs grew heavy. Her breath left her. The world dimmed to a single sound. The slow beating of her own heart.

Above her, the burning circus sank. The sea folded over it without a ripple. The sky went dark.

And in that final darkness, she saw herself reflected—infinite, repeating, each reflection wearing a hat. Each smiling.

Then the dream swallowed itself whole.

Baller sat in the kitchen with his elbows on the table, his hair uncombed, his eyes rimmed with dark from a night without sleep. A cup of coffee cooled untouched before him. The clock above the stove ticked soft and measured, the only sound in the room.

Victor entered a few minutes later. His boots were muddy from checking the yard. He moved heavily, as if each step cost him thought. He poured himself a cup from the pot on the stove, sat across from his son. He reached his hand over and squeezed his wrist.

For a while, neither said anything. The silence between them was thick, not born of comfort, but of mutual exhaustion.

Finally, Baller said, "She had a sort of fit."

Victor's eyes lifted. "When? Last night?"

"Yeah," he nodded. "I stayed with her a good while. She was talking...and...and I couldn't tell whether she was delirious or not. She was so clear, Dad," he paused, "but at the same time...there was something gone about her. She was seeing things. She...she thought I was someone else. And then, well, she just...passed out. I sat with her until dawn."

Victor took a long breath, set his cup down. The sound it made on the table was too loud.

"She's sick," he said. "That's what happens. Fever dreams. She's had them before."

"It's not the fever," Baller said. "Did you see the bruises on her arms? Where are those from? The fever?"

"Baller..." Victor hissed. "We've been through this. Doctors said—"

"The doctors don't know what this is," Baller cut in. "She's slipping away, second by second. We keep pretending it's just nerves. Doctors. Doctors. Doctors. She'll die with that word floating above her head."

"Watch your mouth, son."

Baller turned to look out the window, where the light was paling the glass. Outside, the trees still dripped from the rain.

"We have to find someone."

"And we will," Victor said. "Tomorrow we will find a specialist in the city. We'll take her out together."

"Tomorrow might be too late."

Victor reached across the table, his hand rough and calloused.

"She's not gone yet. We'll do what needs doing, and she'll be well."

Baller nodded slowly, though neither of them believed the reassurance. The house had felt wrong since dawn. A kind of stillness that wasn't peace.

He opened his mouth to say something more when a sound came from the hall. The soft pad of bare feet on linoleum.

India appeared in the doorway. Her hair was still damp from sleep, her face pale beneath the tiredness. She was holding the edge of her robe closed with one hand, the other gripping the doorframe.

She paused at the threshold a moment, twisting her neck to look back towards the living room.

"Victor, where's the girl? Where's Melody?"

Both men turned.

"What do you mean?" Victor asked.

"I mean she's not in bed. Where is she? Did you move her?"

Baller straightened, confusion knitting his brow. "She's not—what? Fords with her."

"Fords in the bathroom. And she's not there."

"You sure?"

"Yes!" she gasped. "I-I thought you moved her. The window's open. I figured you'd opened it to air the room out for her."

Baller bolted out of the room. Victor and India came close behind. At the top of the hall, the door to Melody's room stood half open. Morning light spilled through the gap, pale and cold.

Baller pushed the door wide open.

The bed was empty. The sheets lay tangled, damp with sweat. The pillow had fallen to the floor. The window on the far wall gaped open, its curtains fluttering inward, pale shapes billowing in the draft. Outside, the woods stood silent and wet.

For a long moment, no one moved.

"What's going on?" Ford's voice spilled in. He walked into the gap and saw the empty bed. "Oh my God…"

Victor stepped forward, looking from the bed to the window, as though trying to map some rational path between them. "She couldn't have gone far. She's weak."

"She couldn't have gone anywhere," Ford said. "I was just here a moment ago. She was fast asleep."

Victor went to the window and leaned out. The air smelled of rain and pine. The sill was wet, and along its edge were smudges of dark dirt, faint impressions that might have been fingertips. The ground below showed no clear footprints, only grass pressed down in uncertain shapes.

"Dad," Ford said, his voice small.

Victor didn't answer. He stood beside the bed, his hand on the crumpled blanket. His fingers trembled. The heat was gone from it. It had cooled in mere moments. As if she had never been there at all.

India crossed to the window. The wind lifted her hair.

"I'm calling the police," Baller said.

"Son, wait," Victor stopped him. "Not yet. She's close. I can feel it."

"You can *feel* it?" Baller hissed.

India was already off. She went from corner to corner, calling softly to Melody, as if she might be hiding.

Ford watched her and felt his stomach hollow. He turned back to the window, the woods beyond a wall of green shadow and light. A crow lifted from a branch and flew toward the fields, its cry sharp and solitary.

"I'm not waiting for shit. Are you crazy? I'm calling the cops right now."

Victor said nothing. His hand still rested on the bed. He looked old, older than his boys had ever seen him. The weight of years pressed into the lines of his face, into the slack corners of his eyes.

India sank into the chair by the dresser, her hands shaking.

"What now?" she asked.

Nobody answered.

Time began to stretch and blur. Days uncoiled without shape. The world kept moving but the family did not. The posters went up first — her face printed in grainy ink, the same school photograph that had once hung on the refrigerator door. Her name beneath it in bold black letters. MELODY SOOK. Missing since last Tuesday. Age twenty-six. Last seen near the family home on County Road 17.

The town responded the way small towns always do, with a surge of movement, of purpose, of pity. The volunteers came with dogs and flashlights, with maps spread across the hoods of trucks. The sheriff's men combed the woods and the creek, shouting her name into the trees as if she might answer. Reporters came too, their vans parked along the roadside, their faces solemn before the cameras.

At the Diner, people whispered over coffee cups. Some said she had wandered off in her sleep. Some said she had been taken. Others said it was happening again — that the forest had claimed another one. The name Casey began to surface again, that girl from the college, gone without trace two years before. They remembered the posters, the searches, the way her story had ended in silence. The old fear returned, familiar and heavy, as though it had been waiting for permission to come back.

India could no longer sleep. She sat most nights at the kitchen table, staring at the phone as though willing it to ring. Victor hardly spoke at all. He walked the woods alone with a flashlight, following trails that ended in nothing. The search parties dwindled, the volunteers returned to their lives, but he kept going, long after hope had thinned to habit. He came home each night with mud on his boots, his face blank and gray.

Baller had gone back to the city for a few days. Meetings, he said, though no one believed him. When he returned, his eyes were hollow, his voice quieter than before. He sat at the table with Ford one morning, both men staring at the window, neither saying what they were thinking. The air in the house felt different now, as if something inside it had shifted when she left. Every room seemed to echo her absence.

The phone did ring once, a week after she vanished. It was Vince. His voice came small through the static.

"I heard," he said. "About Melody."

India took the call. She didn't say much, only that they were still looking, that the police had no leads. Vince's voice broke. "She was good," he said. "She deserved better." There was a pause, a breath caught between guilt and grief. "I'm sorry."

India wanted to ask him what he knew, whether he had seen her in the days before, but the words would not come. The line went quiet. When he finally hung up, the silence that followed seemed worse than before.

Later that night, Baller mentioned the call while drying dishes. "Vince reached out," he said simply. Ford nodded, but neither of them spoke the name again. It hung between them, unsaid and heavy, like a wound that could not be looked at directly.

The summer deepened. The posters began to fade under rain and sun, their corners curling, ink bleeding into the paper. The town moved on, as towns must, but the Ward house did not. The garden overgrew, the windows stayed shuttered. Neighbors left food on the porch, small offerings against helplessness. Sometimes India would stand there, staring at the road, half expecting to see her daughter walking up the drive, thin and smiling, saying she had only gone out for air.

Then, two weeks after the last search party, something changed.

It was Ford who found it. He had gone to the sheriff's office to collect some of Melody's things—a scarf recovered near the fence, a small silver ring that had turned up in the grass. The sheriff, a tired man with eyes too soft for his badge, stopped him as he turned to leave.

"There's something else," he said. "Came in this morning. Thought you might want to see."

He led Ford to the back room where a computer screen glowed faintly blue. On it, a grainy video looped, a fixed camera feed from one of the gas stations at the edge of town. The time stamp showed the night she vanished, a little after midnight.

The footage showed the road leading into the woods, dimly lit by a single lamp. For a moment there was nothing, just the dark sway of trees in the wind. Then she appeared.

Melody.

She walked into the frame slowly, her hair loose, her bare feet pale against the asphalt. She was wearing her nightdress, the hem dragging in the dust. Her hands hung loosely at her sides. There was no stumble, no hesitation. She moved as if following a melody only she could hear. Calm. Certain.

The sheriff paused the tape. "That's all we got. The camera cuts out a minute later."

Ford leaned closer to the screen. Her face was turned partly toward the camera. The light caught her eyes, not the color they'd always been, but something else. A faint, unnatural glow. Red, like the dying coal of a cigarette in the dark.

He couldn't speak.

That night, he showed the footage to his parents. They sat together at the table, the laptop open between them. The video played on loop, the same short stretch of road, the same quiet walk. India's hand covered her mouth. Victor watched without blinking.

"She looks…" India began, then trailed off.

"Peaceful," Ford finished.

Victor's jaw tightened. "That's not peace."

The candle flickered beside the screen. The glow from the monitor made the room feel colder. Outside, the wind had picked up again, rustling through the trees. Somewhere beyond them, the forest waited, endless and dark.

When the video ended, no one spoke. They let it replay once more. Each time, the same calm steps, the same faint red shimmer in her eyes. As if she knew where she was going. As if she had been expected.

Baller came in halfway through, returning from the porch. He watched for a moment, then turned away. "Turn it off," he said.

Ford hesitated. "Don't you want to see—"

"Turn it off."

The tone in his voice left no space for argument. Ford closed the laptop. The room went dark except for the candle's flame, small and uncertain.

Victor stood and went to the window. The woods loomed beyond, their shapes black against the rising moon. He could almost imagine her there, walking through the trees, her nightdress brushing against the leaves, her eyes bright and unafraid.

"She looked happy," India said quietly.

Victor didn't turn. "She wasn't happy," he said. "She was gone."

No one said another word. The house fell still again. Outside, the forest shifted—a sound like breath, long and slow, carried on the wind.

EPILOGUE

When she opened her eyes, there was no sky. Only dark, not the kind that ends when the sun comes up, but the kind that goes on forever, a darkness that doesn't need light to know what it is. She lay on a surface that wasn't ground but felt like it. The air was still, heavy, thick with the faint taste of metal. Her body moved slowly, as if underwater.

Something glowed far off, a red light pulsing in the distance. It was enough to show her that she wasn't alone. The shapes came into focus one by one, like stars appearing in reverse: thousands of figures stretching to the horizon, small at first and then growing clearer as the light trembled over them.

The Eggstabletmen.

They stood hunched and still, their ragged clothes fluttering in air that didn't move, their hats low, faces hidden. The red light came from them, from beneath their brims, their eyes burning faint as dying coals. The ground trembled with a low hum, a sound not made by any machine, but by the slow feeding of countless mouths.

Around them, cages rose like towers, bone and wire fused together. Inside, human shapes writhed. They moved without sound at first, then the noise came, thin and distant, a chorus of wailing that never stopped, only changed pitch like wind through a valley.

Melody pushed herself up, her limbs stiff. The light from the creatures stretched across her face, and she realized the air itself shimmered, full of motes that moved like ash. They weren't ash. They were souls-or pieces of them-drifting loose, their faint light dimming as they passed.

The nearest cage hung open. She could see a woman inside, her skin translucent, her face frozen mid-scream. The Eggstabletman beside her held its long fingers at her chest, and light poured from her in threads, pulled out slow, the color of milk. It wasn't blood or vapor, it was memory. Life. She watched the thing draw it into itself, its rags glowing from within.

The woman inside the cage sagged. Her eyes turned to glass. Her body remained, but the part that had made her human was gone. Another century of draining, then she would be filled again, and the cycle would restart. A well that never empties, only forgets what it once held.

Melody stumbled back, her bare feet striking the strange surface, not dirt, not stone, but something that gave slightly under her weight, pulsing faintly. She looked down and saw faces in it, faint, blurred, pushing toward the surface before sinking again.

She whispered, "No."

The sound went nowhere. It was swallowed by the endless hum of feeding. The dark pulsed again. One of the creatures turned toward her. The movement was slow, almost lazy. The hat shifted; the faint line of a mouth appeared beneath the brim.

She recognized him by the shape of the smile.

He moved closer, each step deliberate, careful, like a dancer keeping time to music only he could hear. The other figures didn't react. They went on feeding, their hands working through the motions of eternity.

When he reached her, he spoke without opening his mouth. The words crawled through her mind.

"You're awake at last."

She wanted to run, but her legs wouldn't move. Her body felt pinned to the rhythm of this place. The heat from the ground climbed through her feet into her bones.

He reached out a hand. The nails were long, black, glinting faintly. They weren't claws, they were instruments. Tools for an art she couldn't name.

"This is the real world," he said. "All the others were dreams made to hide this one."

She shook her head. "I killed you."

He laughed softly. "You killed but a dream."

He gestured outward. The horizon rippled, and she saw the full truth, the Eggstabletmen stretching to infinity, each one identical, each feeding, each whispering to the souls in their cages. The sound they made was almost language. Almost a song.

She looked up. Above her was not a sky but a ceiling of water, black and endless. Shapes swam there, human outlines rising and falling like lost swimmers who would never surface. The light from their bodies shimmered briefly before going out.

She wanted to cry, but the tears wouldn't come. There was no water in her here, only light.

The Eggstabletman leaned close. The brim of his hat brushed her forehead. His voice slipped through her skull like a sigh.

"Now, you will dance for me forever."

He lifted a finger and touched her chest. The spot burned, not with pain but with music, a pulse that started small and spread outward. Her body rose from the ground, light spilling from her feet. The surface beneath her pulsed faster, keeping tempo. She felt strings attach themselves to her limbs, invisible, delicate, absolute.

Her legs moved. First a step, then another. The rhythm was familiar. The waltz she had once practiced in her room, alone, believing it was grace. But this was no dance of beauty. This was a ritual   . Every movement fed the thing that watched her. Every turn wrung a little more of her out into the dark.

The other Eggstabletmen began to turn toward her, drawn by the light that bloomed from her body. The feeding stopped. For a moment, there was only silence, a silence full of hunger. Then they began to sway, all of them, thousands of bodies moving in unison, heads tilted, hands rising in imitation of her steps.

The cages shook. The souls inside wailed louder, a symphony of despair. Their sound pressed against her skin, vibrating through her bones. She could feel their lives threading through her, their pain joining hers until she couldn't tell where one ended and the other began.

She screamed then. Not words, just sound, raw, animal, endless. But even that was swallowed by the greater noise, the collective wailing of a thousand lost voices crying into the dark.

Her body kept moving. Her arms lifted, her feet turned. She could feel herself dissolving, light bleeding from her pores, her breath coming apart in sparks. Each movement fed the rhythm. Each spin stole more of her away.

She thought of her brothers, her mother, the house, the trees outside the window. She tried to hold their faces in her mind, but they slipped from her like water through open fingers.

You belong to me now, the Eggstabletman whispered. *You always did.*

She wanted to deny it, but the words stuck in her throat. Her mouth opened and the only sound that came was a low note of the same unending music.

The light within her dimmed. Her soul burned slowly, pulled apart fiber by fiber. The darkness grew thicker, and with each beat of that invisible drum, she lost a little more of herself.

Soon she was no longer sure where her body ended or if she still had one. The world became movement, rhythm, hunger. Around her, the Eggstabletmen swayed, their rags glowing, their mouths smiling. The cages fell silent as the last of the souls were drained.

Above, the ceiling of water rippled once more. She thought she saw daylight beyond it, the faintest suggestion of a sun. But it was only another reflection, another trick of this eternal dark.

And as her final breath turned to light, she saw him watching her, the same soft face, the same small smile.

"Dance," he said.

So, she danced, and the world below the world spun with her.

Trivia

The Eggstabletman

Origins: No single account agrees on where the Eggstabletman first appeared. Some local archives list him as a dream figure seen by fevered children in the 1890s; others trace his name to a mistranslated nursery rhyme about "the man who gathers the shells."

The Hat: Witnesses describe his hat as impossibly deep in shadow, concealing his face except for the faint ridge of his nose and a sliver of mouth that can smile without warmth. In certain folklore, the hat is said to hide *what he has taken*.

The Voice: Always soft. Those who hear it claim the tone adjusts itself to whatever the listener most needs — a teacher's calm, a parent's hush, a lover's whisper.

Dream Rules: He visits in dreams but leaves marks in waking life. Bruises, scratches, or sudden confidence have all been attributed to him.

The Contract: No one remembers agreeing to anything. Yet his "students" all report the same phrase whispered before the end: *You called me first.*

The Other Side

Location: Said to lie beneath the conscious world rather than beyond it. A sub-layer of thought where forgotten dreams go to rot.

Landscape: Early accounts describe a black plain lit by pulses of red light, as if the soil itself breathes. Gravity there seems inconsistent; everything floats slightly, including despair.

Inhabitants: The Eggstabletmen are not born there but arrive through invitation. Each one is believed to represent a single human's reflection their fears given form and patience.

Time: Measured not in hours but in memory. A minute of remembrance above can equal a century below. The trapped are said to relive their most private longings until they become hollow shells.

Exit Theory: No confirmed return has ever been recorded. A fragment from an anonymous diary found near the old woods reads: *"The door is not locked. It only opens inward."*

Architecture/Appearance: The architecture of the Other Side shifts as if built from memory instead of matter. There are no cities, only the suggestion of them; skylines that rise when you look at them and fade when you turn away. Streets form themselves from reflections, paved with glass that remembers footsteps.

The buildings are tall and thin, their walls made of layered veils of shadow, the kind that tremble faintly when you pass. Their windows are not for seeing through but for hearing through: hold your ear against one and you'll catch fragments of the waking world— laughter, weeping, the hiss of traffic—all out of order, as if time itself had been disassembled and left humming.

Bridges hang over nothing. Stairs climb into clouds of dust and never return. Some doorways lead only to a single suspended light bulb, swaying in a draft that has no source. Others open into vast chambers filled with mirrors that do not reflect you but the person you almost became.

The tallest structures are said to be the spires, thin as needles, made from the bones of forgotten moments. They hum when the wind of the black sea passes through them. At their peaks, if one climbs far enough, it's rumored you can see the thin line dividing dream from death — though no one who's reached that height ever came back to describe the view.